a Million aunties

A Million aunties

A NOVEL

Alecia McKenzie

BROOKLYN, NEW YORK

Published by Blouse & Skirt Books and Akashic Books
Blouse & Skirt Books is an imprint of Blue Banyan Books Ltd.
©2020 Alecia McKenzie

ISBN: 978-1-61775-892-8
Library of Congress Control Number: 2020935793

Blue Banyan Books Ltd.
PO Box 5466
Liguanea PO
Kgn 6, Ja
Social Media
Twitter, Facebook, Instagram: @bluebanyanbooks
Website: bluebanyanbooks.com

Akashic Books
Brooklyn, New York
Twitter: @AkashicBooks
Facebook: AkashicBooks
E-mail: info@akashicbooks.com
Website: www.akashicbooks.com

For my mother, Sister Sheena, and Mr. T.

part

one

How to Paint Flowers

The dogs watched him as he trekked up the slope. He expected them to start barking at any moment, yet they remained silent, gazing at him without fear, but with a kind of assessing curiosity. He got the message they were withholding judgment, that they hadn't decided whether he was a friend or someone who meant their mistress harm.

"Strange friggin' dogs," Christopher muttered to himself.

Friggin'. It was a word inherited from his mother and Lidia, both of whom had rarely cursed. Except for this, and the occasional "rass" that burst from his mother when she was annoyed.

Still, if it hadn't been for the dogs, he would've thought the whole area was deserted and would have turned back, retracing his steps on the narrow, stony path that had led him uphill to this place of windowless, soundless houses.

He checked the address again. *Miss Della Robin-*

son, 8 Victoria Street, Port Segovia. It had to be the right place. The three people he'd asked for directions in the town had pointed him this way, trying to conceal their amusement, suppress their questions. "Just go straight up the hill, man. Turn left and then left again. You can't miss it. Victoria Street. Five or ten minutes max." He'd felt them staring after him, as he left the marketplace with the street vendors and their baskets of mangoes and melons.

He arrived after plodding uphill in the sun for more than an hour. And this wasn't much of a street, just a pitted trail teeming with mosquitoes. They were feasting on his ankles, even though he'd taken the precaution of wearing long pants, as Stephen—Miss Della's nephew—had instructed him. "You'll stand out less," Stephen had said. "You might look the look, but people will know you're a foreigner just by the way you walk. Stay away from the shorts for a few days." Good advice, but now he was sweating like a pig, the back of his shirt soaked under the knapsack, the strap of his art portfolio cutting into his right shoulder.

He would have all the quiet he craved at Aunt Della's place, Stephen had promised, while the auntie would gain some cash to fix up her house. Of course, Stephen could easily have paid for whatever renovation was necessary, but his aunt didn't want that, he said. He'd also depicted a yard full of flowers, telling Christopher, "You'll have anything and everything you want. The whole range of tropical beauties: hibiscus, bird of paradise, bougainvillea." But Stephen seemed to have forgotten to describe the emptiness of the area. All the buildings Christopher passed seemed abandoned, their dark interiors lacking any sign of life. They appeared to be waiting for their former occupants to return though; no piles of trash or discarded belongings cluttered the yards, as if someone came frequently to sweep the earth clean, chase away vermin.

Number 8. Hell, could this really be it? The structure was a long, two-storey concrete rectangle. It was unpainted, or, if there had once been paint, it had been sunburned or rain-washed off long ago. The first floor was halfway below the level of the path, while the second floor rose above him. He looked up towards the roof, at the cloudless sky, then down into the yard. More dogs. How many animals did the woman have, for God's sake? He counted them as they gazed at him. Seven. The three who had "greeted" him as he came up the path had joined these four in the yard. Were there more? Maybe the beasts didn't need to bark after all because they were confident no intruder could be a match for them. These weren't scrawny, mangy strays. He could sense their sinews under the healthy-looking fur. They all gleamed different shades of copper, as if they were related. Normally he liked dogs, but he didn't think he'd be stroking these anytime soon.

He drew his phone from his pocket. It might be a good idea to call before venturing down the concrete steps that led from the path, to wherever the front or back door might be. He tapped in the number and held the phone away from his ear, listening for a connecting ring from inside the house. Silence. A burst of obscenities passed through his mind, and he cursed his own stupidity. Why had he thought he needed to come to this godforsaken place to be able to paint? Although, to be fair to himself, he hadn't expected it to be like this. Stephen had said only that it would be quiet and peaceful, that it would be a place of healing and that his aunt made the best breakfasts and dinners. He hadn't mentioned lunch.

"You waiting for me?"

Christopher started, and turned to look at the woman approaching from the opposite direction on the path. She had a broad smile and a friendly, open face, and carried a bulging yellow straw bag in her right hand. She almost matched him for height, her ropy frame in a red–and–black floral sleeveless dress and her greying hair in short thick braids that reached her shoulders. He noticed that her gait was uneven, as if one leg was slightly shorter than the other. It was impossible to guess her age; she could be anywhere between sixty and seventy-five.

"Hi," he said, relief flooding him. "Are you Miss Della?"

"Yes, darling, same one. Stephen tell me bout you. You look like you in need of refreshment."

He grimaced, feeling lightheaded. He sensed movement behind him and saw that the dogs had bounded up, transmitting joy in a paroxysm of tail-wagging. They surrounded Miss Della, doing their excited canine dance, but she shooed them away.

"Stop the foolishness. Go sit down. Come, it's cool inside," she said, turning back to Christopher.

As she spoke, two more dogs raced up from the direction she had come, one tawny like the others and the second a shiny black, with a white stripe down the centre of its face.

"Those two follow me everywhere," she said with a laugh. "Dem stay outside when I go into a shop, to the bank, to the doctor. Stripey been with me the longest, will protect me gainst anything."

They both looked at the striped-faced dog. He was standing stiff-legged, starting to growl. Before Christopher could respond to what Miss Della had said, the dog sprinted toward him, snarling. Christopher froze, and the animal rushed past, chasing something down the slope.

"Lawd, that dog see duppy everywhere. Him soon come back. A spirit musta followed you up the hill."

She chuckled, but her words chilled the sweat running down Christopher's back.

She led him down the steps, taking each with caution.

"Were you at the doctor now?" Christopher asked. "Is everything okay?"

"Yes, everything fine, man. I just went into town to get a few supplies cause I know you coming. Nothing wrong with me except a little arthritis problem in mi right hip."

He felt this wasn't the whole truth but knew it wouldn't be right to pry.

"Can't get around as much as I used to," she continued. "The doctor say walking helps, but the legs is always the first to go when you getting old. And he say I should do yoga, so every morning I stretching but don't ask me if that helping. You know anything bout yoga?"

"I try to stretch too every morning before I start working. Maybe I can show you some postures that might help." But he immediately regretted the words. The last thing he wanted was chattiness first thing in the morning.

"Oh, that would be lovely," Miss Della said. "You know, I can still touch mi toes, even at my age."

He was tempted to ask how old she was but knew the question would be impertinent. If she wanted him to know, she would've mentioned it. Stephen had warned him to watch his language, and to never forget the "Miss" or "Auntie" because people like Miss Della could get stony-faced fast if you addressed them by their first name. Christopher hadn't bothered to tell Stephen that he'd already learned this cultural lesson a long time ago. As for her age, he'd get the details from Stephen when he returned to New York. He'd made a vow not to email anybody during his time on the island, and he didn't suppose Miss Della had Wi-Fi anyway. He wondered if there was even electricity, although the stove on one side of the cavernous kitchen where they now stood seemed to be an electric one. Miss Della set her bag down on a square table covered with a white linen tablecloth that sported golden, embroidered seashells around the hem. He stared at the glass vase with the yellow flowers in the middle of the table, noticing the transparency of the petals; he looked away.

"Come into the living room," Miss Della said before he could remove his knapsack. From the shadows of the kitchen, he followed her into a room bathed in light, and he exhaled sharply at the view.

"Wow!" His reaction was spontaneous. "Nice room." He set his portfolio case down and helped her to push open the French windows before stepping onto the balcony fronting the length of the living room, his knapsack still on. Below, the town stretched to the sea and he could see to the horizon, while on his left the hills rippled in shades of emerald. He mentally began mixing paints and composing an outline, then checked himself. He wasn't there to paint pretty landscapes, post-card scenes.

He turned back to the room, watching Miss Della fluff up cushions on the red three-seater sofa and on the two matching armchairs arranged in front of the outsized flat-screen TV. She must have electricity, unless this was just for decoration. She saw him looking at the television, nodded. "Present from Stephen. He had to grease a few palms to have it pass Customs. But when him set him mind to something, nothing can stop him. I told him I wanted a nice TV, and two months later, him fly in with this."

Christopher smiled in recognition. That was Stephen. Agent, facilitator, man who gets things done and never takes no for an answer. Christopher had once asked him where his unrelenting energy came from and he had given credit to the woman here in this luminous room. "When I was growing up, her favourite commandment was 'find a way' when I said I couldn't do something. Used to drive me nuts."

Christopher had never deciphered the exact relationship between Stephen and his "Aunt Della." On a single occasion, after consuming too much rum, Stephen had mumbled something about his aunt getting him from a place called Anfields Children's Home in Kingston. She'd taken him to the country to help her grow plants and told everyone he was her nephew, and it had gone from being a lie to being true. Stephen didn't mention his parents, and never returned to the subject.

"Your room upstairs," Miss Della said. "But first, come drink some lemonade, and then you can go freshen up."

"Where do the dogs sleep?" he asked.

"Well, usually dem have your room," she answered, with a burst of laughter. "No, I'm joking. Dem stay in the yard. Or if it raining too much, I let dem in the kitchen."

Christopher made a note to avoid the kitchen in the event of a downpour.

Since Lidia had gone, he'd found it even harder to fall asleep. Before, when he used to lie beside her, with his eyes wide open for hours until he got up and did a quick sketch to unwind, she had blamed coffee—which she herself never touched, preferring her herbal teas.

"You know, Chris, if you switched to tea, you'd fall asleep much more easily."

"It's better than before though. I think your yoga is helping. It used be like three o'clock before I even got into bed."

"I'd be a wreck if I did that."

"Well, that's why I never get up before eight," he'd said. "This is one guy who won't catch any worms."

She'd laughed, the sound cheering him as it usually did. When they were in a public place, eating out or riding the bus, and she laughed, people would look in her direction, searching for the source of a song.

He hadn't touched coffee since her funeral, yet he was still lying awake, begging for sleep. At some point between fatigue and loss of consciousness, Lidia came to him, as she'd done since the night of her "farewell ceremony"—that's what her mother called it, her father had said nothing throughout. She was standing, smiling, surrounded by the flowers she had so loved; in the distance, Christopher could hear Stripey barking his stupid head off.

He'd never understood it. How a woman with a PhD in financial economics could opt to be a public gardener, working in the city's parks. Whenever the subject came up, she always said it was because of 9/11, seeing the Twin Towers go down in smoke and dust, then the senseless war later.

"Lost my faith in both religion and finance. Found flowers," she told him. And when others came to know her and asked the same question, she paraphrased Confucius, substituting "woman" for "man" and "husband" for "wife": "If you want a woman to be happy for five years, give her a husband. If you want a woman to be happy for ten years, give her a dog. If you want a woman to be happy for a lifetime, give her a garden. Or in my case, a huge park to take care of."

He told her he was sure Confucius never said anything of the sort. But she said it didn't matter. "Even if it's not true—it sounds nice, right?"

She'd been promoted several times since she'd switched professions and could have stayed in her office, gazing at the Brooklyn skyline. But she insisted on being on the ground, pushing a wheelbarrow and planting, dressed in green overalls like her staff. He would meet her sometimes for lunch, and they'd sit on a bench, eating takeout health food—tofu, lentils and wild rice, or some such—while the flowers she'd planted waved in the breeze as if from an impressionist's canvas.

"Have you ever tried painting flowers?" she asked him once. And he'd laughed. He knew the subjects he could paint, and flowers weren't among them. But, yes, he had tried, many times, and the damn things had come out looking like evil birds, or mangled rolls of toilet paper, and he had to admit he didn't have that delicacy of touch that made petals look like petals.

His sophomore art teacher in college had tried to teach him that lightness of stroke. He'd never forgotten her—miss moon shine. That was how she signed her work, all in lowercase letters. She would bend over him, take his brush, and apply a quick dash of white. She said all the masters knew how to paint flowers and considered it her duty to teach him and the rest of the class how to portray everything from calla lilies to lilacs.

"Painting flowers is political action," she told him as she flicked titanium white on his canvas, capturing the light as he never could. "When people bully you, you paint flowers. When they burst into your house and shoot at your family, you paint flowers. When they tell you that you shouldn't be an artist but a basketball player, you paint flowers."

She shoved the brush down into his plastic tub of water and strode away to another student, while he swallowed the comment he wanted to shout—that he'd signed up for art and not a frigging philosophy course. How had she known that his future had been mapped out as a basketball star? Did he somehow project the disappointment he'd seen on his father's face after he'd declared he had no intention of playing professionally, no matter the high-school sports prizes he'd won?

He always felt the urge to give a sarcastic retort to miss moon shine's little soliloquies, but whenever she leaned over him, her straight black hair brushing his face as she corrected a line or added colour, his breath caught in his throat. He also realised he couldn't best her in wordplay, so he was better off not even trying. She was one of those teachers who walked into the classroom with a don't-mess-with-me attitude. And if her grammatical mistakes might have caused hilarity, no one laughed at that because her wit was the sharpest in the department. Unwary students had seen their smart-mouth attempts boomerang, and he wasn't about to join them.

"Really? You don't like Monet? I don't give a shit. Learn to paint like him first and then you can forget his ass later," she told them. It seemed that no one at the school had informed her that teachers shouldn't swear.

The only thing he and the others knew about her was that she'd come from a place called Changsha in Hunan Province. She'd arrived in the States when she was fourteen, knowing only "hello" and "zank you"—that was how she pronounced it when she told them the story—and she'd taught herself English staying up nights throughout high school. Now she had an MFA, and if they didn't believe she knew what she was talking about, they could shift their asses out of the classroom right this minute.

They had no idea if she was married, had children, or went back home on holiday. But word was that she had a famous agent and that her work sold in London and Paris, in addition to New York. And maybe in Changsha too, which Christopher had checked on a map, knowing it wasn't a place he was likely to visit.

The other students thought that he was her favourite, and they teased him about it outside of class. Inside, miss moon shine mocked him for his fear of using white.

"Why you so afraid of white?" she asked. "When you paint, all you're doing is showing light, and you need white colour for that."

One of his friends in the class, Gavin—a dedicated basketball player taking the course as an elective—burst out, "Tell her why you so afraid of white. Tell her it's something primeval for all of us." His laughter boomed through the class, as other students bent lower over their work.

Miss moon shine stared at Gavin. "Me too. I was scared of white, but that wasn't going to stop me. What don't kill you make you strong."

"Really?" Gavin muttered. "Easy for you to say."

"No," miss moon shine responded. "Not easy for me to say." The way she enunciated the words caused the temperature in the class to drop, and no one said anything else.

Gavin was now in the NBA, following his own primeval need to earn loads of money. "No starving in a fucking attic for me," he'd said when the subject of art as a career came up. Yet, he'd been the best artist in miss moon shine's class. She'd said so herself, aloud, at the end, but that hadn't swayed Gavin from his path. He told Christopher he'd only signed up for the course because he'd heard that nude models were coming to pose, and Christopher suspected this was a rumour miss moon shine had spread herself so that not only girls would take Introduction to Painting.

Once the dollars started rolling in, Gavin bought three of Christopher's canvases, works that miss moon shine would've considered too dark, and violent. He'd also collected half a dozen of miss moon shine's flowers.

Christopher had kept in touch with her for a few years after he graduated, and then the correspondence had dwindled to nothing. In one of his last messages, he'd asked her if "moon shine" was her real name. And she'd replied, "It doesn't matter. When you try to paint the moon, just focus on the shine. Light is everything. They used to call me Alice when I was growing up." Typical bullshit. Why couldn't she have just answered the question?

He found out years later from Google that her birth name was Li Ying and that she was still teaching and painting, though she had neither Facebook nor Twitter accounts—something Stephen had forced him to have, despite his contempt for social media. "No ignoring it in this day and age," his friend and agent stressed over and over, but miss moon shine obviously did.

When he'd told Lidia about her, and her obsession with light, Lidia had agreed that his paintings were overly dark. She even wondered audibly at times if they reflected some hidden anger. In their occasional heated quarrels, she had more than once snarled, "Go take it out on your frigging canvas and leave me alone."

The darkness he portrayed connected with other viewers though, because his paintings sold, and sold well. He had Stephen to thank for some of it, but the rest was because of his talent. He wasn't shy about admitting that. And Lidia recognized his skill even if she didn't like all the paintings that hung in their loft apartment. To amuse her, and perhaps send a message to miss moon shine—if she ever came across his work, he'd started adding a random flower in the corner of his ominous cityscapes. Lidia laughed when she saw the first one, but she'd still thought he had a long way to go.

He wondered what she would've made of the

paintings he did after her burial. Each stroke had felt as if he were stabbing her killers, slashing them to pieces. Except they were already dead. Blew themselves up afterwards. Each time he thought of them, the ball in his chest grew harder.

He'd painted for days. And got up at night to continue. Until he could no longer raise his right arm, and a bump bulged at his wrist. His doctor diagnosed tendinitis, sending him to an osteopath, but he ignored the exercises prescribed. Afterwards, with his left hand, he shredded the canvases he'd completed, while the two artists he shared his studio with looked on in panic, wondering what to do. When he had finished hacking, he slumped to the floor, sitting with his legs wide open like a child.

One of the artists, Féliciane, rushed for her mobile and called Stephen.

"Do you think this is what Lidia would've wanted?" Stephen asked him that night. And for the first time since her funeral, Christopher cried. He wanted to tell Stephen about the other thing he'd done, after the police called him to the morgue to identify Lidia's limbless body. But the shame stopped him.

He wasn't aware he'd slept until the soft knock came at the door. He opened his eyes and squeezed them back shut against the glare flooding the room. He'd have to ask her to do something about the curtains.

"Yes?"

"It's me," Miss Della said. "What time you want your breakfast? Or we going to exercise first?"

"What time is it?"

"Six thirty," she said cheerfully. He groaned in response. Like nephew, like aunt. Stephen was always sending him phone messages at dawn, messages he saw only hours later because he'd begun turning off his phone when he and Lidia went to bed.

"Does that blasted man ever sleep?" Lidia had asked. "You two should be roommates."

Except that wouldn't have worked. Christopher went to bed late and slept long, while Stephen did the opposite.

"Okay. I'm getting up," he told Miss Della through the door. "I'll be down in a minute."

He lay in bed for another ten minutes or so, looking at the ceiling and the patterns on the faded white paint. Miss Della needed a new roof. She'd shown him the buckets in the corners of the bedroom the evening before, telling him where to place them when it rained.

He eased off the mattress and shuffled down the corridor, his forty-four years feeling like eighty. One bathroom was at the end of the hall and the other en suite from Miss Della's room. She had given him a tour of the place yesterday evening, showing him the four bedrooms upstairs, in addition to the living and dining areas below. He splashed cold water on his face, knowing that the tap for warm water didn't work. If he wanted a hot shower, he'd have to heat up water in the electric kettle, add it to cold water in a basin, and pour it over himself, Miss Della had told him. It wasn't worth the trouble.

He changed out of the shorts he'd slept in and put on light loose pants of Indian cotton that Lidia had bought. She'd said he looked "manly" in the orange-and-black triangular patterns, but he'd never worn the pants in public. Downstairs, Miss Della was already on the balcony, wearing a mauve tee-shirt and matching jogging trousers, twisting her torso from left to right. He joined her and began doing the same movements.

"You ever play basketball?" Miss Della asked, as he leant forward to show her the sun salute. It was the first posture Lidia had taught him, one Saturday morning in Prospect Park.

"Yes, in high school. You?"

She stretched her arms up, and her laugh tinkled. "Well, I used to play netball long-long time ago. It wasn't something for a career though. When I leave high school, I work for a bit doing accounts. Then a few things happen here and there, and I decide to go into the nursery business."

"You mean taking care of kids?" He wondered if that was how Stephen had come into her life.

"No, taking care of plants. Growing and selling them."

"Oh." He felt his chest constricting.

He and Lidia had no choice but to meet. She grew up in Firenze, Italy, her mother Italian and her father Iranian. And he was born in Firenze, Alabama, his mother Jamaican and his father American—a Vietnam vet who refused to eat the rice and peas his wife so loved. "I ate enough rice during the war to last a lifetime," his father would say. Christopher had spent his first twelve years in Firenze, near the famed Beta Shoals studio where fading soul singers came to revive their careers with a last-chance recording. Millie J., Bobby Mack, these were some of the names who'd created dream songs there, his father told him. It wasn't until his family moved to New York and he was in high school that he'd realised another Firenze existed, a place of different masterpieces.

Yet they hadn't met in either of the Firenzes, but in a Brooklyn park. He'd gone there to sketch, not flowers but the cityscape behind the cherry blossom trees—making the outlines jagged and threatening as he did. He'd been immersed in his work, unmindful of the woman looking over his shoulder at his rapid hand movements, the black lines jumping off the paper. He was used to passersby stopping to have a look when he worked outdoors.

"Nice," she said.

They all said that.

He glanced up and then looked again, struck by the face above the olive green of the park uniform, the wide almond-shaped eyes with the translucent brown pupils, and the curly black hair escaping from its bun. Maybe she was on some kind of photo shoot?

"So you're an artist," she said, stating the obvious.

"Hmmm, and you?"

"I guess I'm a gardener, or maybe a flower grower, plant caretaker, or something like that. Official title: landscape architect."

So, not a model. She looked too down-to-earth and smart for that, he thought, while at the same time scolding himself for his prejudice.

He chatted with her as he continued sketching, and they discovered they were both Firenzines, which became a running joke from then on. It wasn't until weeks later that he found out she was "Dr. Zarin," with a PhD in financial economics from Columbia Business School.

"Why did you stop playing basketball?" Miss Della asked as they did the final posture, each supine on the beach towels she had brought out.

"I'll tell you later. Just concentrate on your breathing for now."

"Hmm mmm," Miss Della said. "But why?"

"Didn't enjoy it anymore. Art was more interesting. Up until now." He sighed.

She said nothing else, and he listened to the whisper of their breath, in and out in unison.

Miss Della had already prepared fried dumplings with ackee and saltfish for breakfast. Now she began frying the slices of plantain that she'd left covered on a plate. The smells brought back his mother's cooking, and he felt the instant connection, the slide to childhood. His mother had embraced her American life, but never the food. Her cooking bridged the space between her and the island, filling his nostrils with scents of a place that seemed farther away than it was. As if smell and taste should suffice, she had taken him "home" only once when he was growing up—information that Stephen had greeted with disbelief.

"You went only once? Only once?"

And he tried to explain that when you lived in Firenze, you couldn't really be American and something else. You had to choose your identity, as his mother had done, for herself and for him, except for the food. Before flying to the island now, he had told his father where he was going, and the old man had been surprised. "Your mother would've liked that," was all he said.

Like Miss Della, his father now lived alone, but that was the extent of the similarity. In the six years since his mother died, ending the onslaught from breast cancer, his father had grown more sullen and withdrawn. Only Lidia had been able to make his face glow. And he was getting forgetful too, repeating the same line he'd said five minutes before. Christopher knew how much his father missed Lidia, especially her laughter, but since the funeral, they hadn't referred to what had happened.

Before Christopher left this time, his father asked him once again when he planned to come and collect the boxes of soul albums he had sorted for him, and Christopher sighed. "When I come back, Dad. I promise."

He paid the wife of the building's caretaker to check on his father every day and prepare his meals. And he gave her Stephen's number too, just in case. He hoped she wouldn't need it.

While Miss Della fried her plantains, the burnt-honey smell filling the kitchen, Christopher looked out the window at the yard. The dogs—in various stages of somnolence—eyed him back. Only Stripey stood tense, staring at him with an unnerving look of expectation.

"Why do you have so many dogs? For protection?"

"Only two is really mine, the one-dem that follow me everywhere," she answered. "The rest come here after the landslide."

"Landslide?"

"Yes, bout seven months ago, after all the rain. Hurricane season, you know? So everybody have to leave, the government say it was better. Normally people would ignore the fool-fool politician-dem, but a little bwoi die when it happen, and even though people might risk dem own life, dem not going to take chances when it come to dem pickney."

"So, where did they go?"

"All over. Some just in town. You didn't see the new house-dem, like little box? Other people gone farther away."

"And you stayed?"

"Yes, the house okay, as you can see. Just the leaks."

He looked round the kitchen, at the pots on the thick wooden shelf that ran high along one wall and the mugs on the hooks underneath. The shapes made him compose a painting in his head. That had always been his thing. Shapes, not flowers—something even miss moon shine had come to understand. She'd told him that his future might lay in graphics, or architecture.

"Does Stephen know?" he asked.

"Not everything," Miss Della answered, without looking up. "Just that it rain hard, and a few of the plant-dem get wash way, and the house leaking here and there. No need for worry."

She told him where to find knives and forks, and he set them on the table. When she brought the heaped plates over, he realised why Stephen hadn't said anything about lunch.

After breakfast, he accompanied her with the dogs along the other side of the path from which he'd ascended and discovered that here was a shortcut down the hill, to the town, with a less steep incline. From the tyre marks, he realised that cars could come up to the street this way. He could've taken a taxi from the market square yesterday after the minibus from the airport had dropped him off in town, if only he'd paid better attention to Stephen's directions.

Miss Della showed him where her nursery had been—a plot now occupied by weeds and mosquitoes.

"They say you should build your house on high ground, but nobody ever tell you bout landslides, right?" She laughed without humour. "Thank goodness I had enough save up to start over, and Stephen always such a big help. Don't know what I would do without him."

The new nursery was on flat ground, on land she rented from her doctor. As they walked, trailed by the two canine bodyguards, she told him how she'd cried after the landslide. Not only because of the child lost and the damage to her neighbours' homes, but because of the plants and flowers swept away.

Christopher listened and felt the ball in his chest getting bigger, weightier. After the attack in the park—

which had killed women, children at play, and three city employees tending the flowerbeds—people had been further outraged at the destruction in the city's gardens that they'd woken up to a day later. Someone had gone on a rampage, ripping up plant after plant, trampling petals into the earth. It had outraged people, who spoke and posted about it for days. To Christopher, it had seemed they valued plant life more than human life. But now he guessed it was what the destruction symbolized that had so horrified the city's residents. They thought the two attacks were linked, that the second was like pissing on someone after creeping up and knifing them in the back.

A smooth-skinned woman in her forties and an older man, both wearing khaki shirt and pants, greeted them at the nursery, exchanging jokes with Miss Della.

"So, who is your handsome young friend?" the woman teased.

"I bring him for you, Lorraine," Miss Della replied, and the younger woman laughed, shooting Christopher a flirtatious look. But he could see it was just a game. He noted the thick, expensive-looking gold ring on her left hand, screaming out her status to the world.

He shook hands with the man, whom Miss Della introduced as Mr. Jordan. "Him is the best farmer round here, best orange, lime, and everything, but he come sometimes just to help me out." Mr. Jordan smiled at her with what Chris saw as deep affection.

The nursery already had more than thirty different species, Miss Della told him proudly as he followed her, and the place was still growing. She led him between the rows of potted plants, pointing out yellow bells, anthurium, and amaryllis. She asked which ones he preferred.

He selected the yellow bells, their golden tones contrasting with the glazed sea-green of the ceramic pot. He would start with this.

They got into a rhythm over the next days. He learned to get up early and help her feed the dogs. Afterwards they exercised on the balcony before the sun was fully up, and followed this with the big breakfast, washing down plantains, callaloo, and mackerel with sweetened mint tea.

When she left to go to the nursery, with Stripey and pal in tow, he set up his portable easel in the yard, placing the flowers on a folding table she had provided. The remaining dogs watched him as he worked, tensing when he cursed at a wrong stroke. He knew they were warming to him though; the wagging of tails wasn't far off.

It was like learning all over again as he tried to capture the flowers on the canvas board. But he would keep at it, day after day, until he got it right, until he could depict that light miss moon shine always wanted, the light Lidia had brought. He could feel her at his shoulder, at ease with Stripey gone. She hadn't asked this of him, but he needed to do it, so they could both find peace.

He would stay months if he had to, sitting among

Miss Della's dogs, until he had enough paintings to equal the plants he'd destroyed that night he'd run amok in Lidia's gardens, ripping roots from the soil, tramping through the flowerbeds, like an animal gone mad from a shot that should have put it down. He'd felt blinding rage at the garden, those flowers, that hadn't protected her.

He hoped she forgave him. Now.

"Nice," she said, looking over his shoulder, and her laugh rang out.

CHAPTER TWO

LPs and Drawings

I hope Christopher comes soon for the records. I've packed them up and they're waiting for him in the back room. More than three hundred of them. Three hundred and thirteen to be exact. Eight from Percy Sledge alone. Yeah, he could sing. And five from Johnny Mayhew—Eileen bought those. I never could stand that too-suave voice. Like he'd never felt pain. But she adored him. When he came on TV, staring into the camera with his doe-like eyes, lashes as long as a girl's, I always felt like switching the channel, but I indulged her instead. The other day I saw a youngish man on ABC who looked just like Johnny. Turned out it was his son. Who would've thought!

I guess Chris will chuck the Mayhew LPs out. I hope he'll keep Percy and Otis and James. And Millie. I can't remember when I stopped listening to them. One day I had to hear the music, it made me feel so much better, and the next, I couldn't bear it. The silent house was easier than the memories.

Percy Sledge was on the car radio when Eileen and I drove from Firenze to Waterloo for our first date, if I can call it that, a picnic by the lake. I wasn't on the road long before I noticed the car, a sheriff's patrol, trailing us. I kept driving at a normal speed in the Falcon, while the car behind kept the same distance. When we parked by the lake, he parked too. When we got out, he stayed in the car. Watched us as we spread a blanket, laid out the chicken, greens, and rice and peas Eileen had prepared. She didn't know then how much I hated rice. We'd met just three weeks before, five months after I got back from Nam, and there was still a lot to discover about each other.

The jackass in his khaki hat and uniform sat while we had our picnic, looking at us through his car window as if we were rare birds, or maybe the ghosts of Indians come back to haunt Waterloo. They'd had to pass this way when they got forced onto reservations, right? Trail of Tears. Marching, marching with so many falling by the way. I wouldn't have been surprised if the jackass had taken out binoculars, or a rifle. I tried not to be nervous, but Eileen was simply annoyed. She hadn't grown up here, hadn't been in the country long enough yet. She wanted to go over and give him a piece of her mind, ask him what he thought he was playing at. No sheriffs sitting in cars watching people in Kaya Bay, where she came from.

"Maybe I should just go and offer him some rice and peas," she said. I couldn't help it, I had to laugh. That was the thing that drew me to Eileen. She made

America funny. But a long time later, when she kept smiling, calling the racists "fools," it only made me irate. It was as if she couldn't see beyond the foolishness, to the wickedness. You can't just laugh at everything, no matter how you see history, I used to tell her. And she would make that sound I grew to know too well, the infuriating one, kissing her teeth. "They not going to turn me into what they want" was her mantra. "Nobody changing me to fit their own stupidity." She pronounced it "chew-pidity." Deliberately. To show where she came from. We would argue then, about race, of all things. Arguing, when she should have been in full agreement with me.

"The thing with you and your people, Herb, is that you keep on hoping the country will change and that one day they'll start loving you," she declared. "They not going to change. So you might as well just live your life—enjoy what America has to offer, and ignore them."

That got me really worked up. Easy to say if you don't have anybody to ignore, I told her, but when they're there all the time and one wrong move on your part could see you in jail or in the morgue, then it's a different matter.

But there was no sense arguing with her. She was always right. The arrogance and confidence of growing up as a majority. The shortsightedness of it.

She got truly angry once, though, in '83, but I'll come to that.

Chris is more like her than me, imbibing her "don't let them define you" rubbish, as if that would save him when a sheriff pushed him against a wall. He acts as if he's from the other side. Take the art thing. I don't even want to get into that now. He could've been like Magic or Michael, could've taken care of his mother and me, not that I would've ever asked him for anything. But Eileen was always: let him do what he wants to do. Except some of us don't have that luxury.

If I could've done what I wanted to do, I would have walked over to that sheriff that September Sunday and dragged him from his power-bubble. I would have smashed him to the ground and kicked him until he screamed for his momma.

But we can't all go around doing as we wish. Eileen and I finished our picnic. I acted like I wasn't rushing when we wrapped things up and put the basket and blanket in the trunk. I wanted to be out of Waterloo before the sun began going down.

He trailed us the twenty-two miles back to Firenze. I turned the radio up high, and Eileen and I sang along to "When a Man Loves a Woman."

I haven't been back to Waterloo since. I heard that the sheriff there is now black and the mayor is a woman—for the second or third time. When we lived in Firenze, Waterloo had maybe three hundred people, all lily white. To get there and to Pickwick Lake, you'd have to drive along a narrow road, with the Tennessee River on one side and woods on the other, hiding the houses. A few years after our picnic, my homeboy Les was out there late one evening, I have no idea why, and his car broke down in the darkness. He couldn't get it to start. So he ventured through the woods, praying the whole time, and knocked on the door of the first house he came to. A white man, about sixty, opened the door, stared at him, and asked what he wanted. When Les explained, the man went back into the house and came out with tools and a flashlight. He followed Les to the car. Looked at the engine and said the radiator was overheating. He opened the cap and let off the steam, and they stood side by side just staring at the metal workings. When Les got on his way, he looked in the rearview mirror and saw the man standing there in the road with his flashlight. Les was trembling.

We all thought he was damn lucky, especially because Les is 6'2", and people like to feel intimidated by tall people. When a bunch of us, me and Les and others, used to walk home after high-school team practise, we'd get jittery stares, although everyone guessed we were basketball players. But that's the thing with crackers, you never know how they'll behave on any given day. And you just don't know when you'll meet one who's burning with hatred for everybody, but mostly for you.

Firenze had its share of them, but they never would've done anything like in Birmingham or Selma. You got the looks and the words, ever so often, but not the crimes. Things had changed by the time I got back from Nam anyway and a lot of us were getting on okay. It seemed people were closer than before I left, like some were really trying, sorry for things that had happened in the past. Maybe cussing against the war had united them, or all the assassinations, I don't know.

The thing was, nobody wanted to hear my views, or what I'd been through. Not that I would've talked about it, if they asked. My two sisters Ella and Doreen were teachers, like Momma had been, sharing a nice house on Maple, and most of their friends had decent jobs and nice sports cars. On Sunday, everyone went to church and held up those the spirit took, or made sure they got the spirit themselves and began with the shaking and wailing. I went a few times after I got back and then stopped going. But that's where I met Eileen. Call it Divine will.

The pastor had asked Eileen out a couple of times before she went out with me, and maybe that's why I got the distinct impression that I was no longer welcome in his House of Worship. Pastor Samuels was a divorced man, with an eight-year-old son, and I think he was looking among the flock for a stepmother for his boy. Eileen would've been a fine choice. She had one of those smiles, the kind that people with good teeth like to flash, and she was always in a dress. I soon learned that she was staying with an aunt, over on Chestnut, who was a dressmaker, able to make clothes from scratch—even entire suits, jackets and all. This aunt had filed for Eileen to come to the States, when Eileen's mother passed from cancer, and there she was now, amidst us by the Tennesee River, in the Shoals.

"Did your aunt choose this area because of all the water?" I asked Eileen. I figured that to live in Kaya Bay or anywhere on an island, you'd learn to love the sea, rivers, any kind of water.

"No, she just met a man who came from the South. He was a tourist. They moved here so they could be together."

Turned out that her aunt's husband, the late Uncle Tommy, was born white. He pretended for years to be a light-skinned black man, the only time in my life up until then I'd ever heard of that. He always shaved his head close to the scalp, Eileen said, until he went bald and it wasn't necessary anymore. Tommy had come from Troy, down near Montgomery, and they chose Firenze on a whim after they drove through on their way north. Nobody knew him here. Nobody suspected. So he just recreated his life so they could live together without hassle from racists. Eileen told me this as if it was the cutest thing in the world, like an Anansi scam.

Anansi the spider. When Chris was little, Eileen used to tell him these stories all the time. Once upon a time, she went, Anansi was hungry, very very hungry, but so were his wife and their three children. They kept bawling and rubbing their empty bellies. Anansi had no choice but to head out in search of food. But first he looked through his closet for his best clothes and put on his one suit and tie. He knew that if he looked poor, people wouldn't give him much, because they would just think he wasn't used to having anything. But if he looked wealthy, people would think, *Oh, poor man, down on his luck. Let me help him.* So all dressed up, Anansi went from farm to farm and spun tales about being temporarily out of money and needing to feed his family. Everyone who listened to him felt moved, and they put bananas, oranges, mangoes, yam, plantains, and all kinds of food into his basket. He raced home later, handing over everything to his wife and kids. As they dug in, he sat there eating nothing himself. So, they all felt sorry for him, and each gave him half of what was on their plate. Anansi of course ended up with the biggest share, which he somehow always managed to do. He smacked his lips and grinned as he ate. Tomorrow he would have to think of a different trick.

I didn't know what she was trying to teach Chris with these stories, so I just kept my mouth shut. I wondered if her Aunt Veronica had told Tommy some Anansi tales before he decided on his lifelong transformation. But as Eileen said, *to each his own.* Everyone who knew him said Tommy had been a good man.

Anyway, there was Eileen, a bird of paradise on the water. My sisters laughed that it was a wonder I hadn't come home with a Vietnamese. But here I was, still going foreign.

I loved the dresses she wore, all made by her Aunt Veronica, all with a fitted cut and tasteful colours— black and red, lime green, burgundy. And never above the knees. I can't remember ever seeing her in pants that whole time. Dresses made her feel freer, she said. With her petite frame, she sometimes looked like a doll.

Just a week after arriving in Firenze, she'd found a job as a receptionist with Stanley White, owner of White's Funeral Home, and that's where she was working when we met. Stanley was the richest black man in town. He knew how to get money out of you even before you were ready to pass to the other side. I would laugh when I went to pick up Eileen sometimes after work and see the sign he had put up in big bold black letters: *Inquire about our new prepaid, prearranged funeral plan*.

Stanley was short, round, and balding, an alligator in business but a poodle in private apparently. Eileen said he gave away a lot of his money, for scholarships. That kind of thing. And she could always count on a bonus during a good month of funerals. He sometimes invited us for a barbecue at his house—a two-storey place with a huge yard in front and back, across the bridge from Firenze, in the Shoals itself. He probably had a good view of the river from the second floor, but we were never invited upstairs. His wife, Ursuline, was a head taller, and half his width, with a striking crown of straightened hair, or maybe a wig, now I come to think of it. She had a booming laugh that rang through the neighbourhood. Another woman with excellent teeth, though hers seemed bought. They were all too even, too ivory. When you have crooked front teeth yourself, you notice these things. I felt she and Stanley were good folks, yet there was something that told you not to get too close. Maybe it was the smell of death-wealth hanging over the place. And I wondered why they needed such a big house, when it was just the two of them. No kids.

We hadn't seen Stanley for years after we left Firenze, and then he turned up at Chris's first big show, in Brooklyn. For some reason, Eileen had sent him an invitation and since he was going to be in town anyway—a morticians' convention—there he was.

"Still so beautiful! You haven't changed a bit," he told Eileen, wrapping her in a hug that went on for too long. They were both exactly the same height.

"Nor you, Mister Stanley," she answered. "You look younger than when I was working for you." He beamed like the moon, turning to shake my hand and looking me up and down. I guess I didn't look that great because he didn't comment on my appearance. His head barely reached my shoulder, and I pulled myself up to be even taller.

"You must be so proud of your son," he said, looking over to where Chris was standing, talking with the gallery owner. "Art was something I always wanted to do, back in the day."

Fancy that, I thought. *And instead you make dead bodies look beautiful.* "Yeah. I am. Proud," I said out loud.

"I always knew Chris would do great," he went on. "I could see the talent from back then."

Sometimes, when Eileen still had work to do, she would take Chris to the funeral home after school, and he would entertain himself by drawing everything in sight, which was mostly coffins. It seems good old Stanley had been tickled to bits that Chris liked to portray his shiny, expensive caskets. He even gave him advice on how to make them look more realistic. This I was hearing for the first time.

Stanley bought the most expensive painting in the exhibition, a huge rectangle with a lot of thick black

lines. Perfectly suitable for a mortician's home. "Ursuline will love it," he said, and I could see his wife's
perfect false teeth gleaming as her laugh echoed up the
East Coast.

After Stanley left, I gave Chris's paintings another look.
If someone was willing to spend that kind of money,
maybe I was missing something.

From the moment your kid comes into the world,
you start building dreams for them in your head, start
wanting them to become what you maybe couldn't. I
can only think this now. I wasn't conscious of it before.
Chris was born a year and a half after Eileen and I got
married and by then the VA had found me a job as a
sound engineer at the recording studio, where everybody who was a true professional came. I'd got training
for radio work in the military, for dealing with mikes
and dials, making sure a sound was as clean as it could
be. I wanted my singers, as I called them, to sound better
than anybody else on the radio. Millie was one of the
most demanding regulars, but I didn't mind when she
flashed her long, red, false nails, stared out from under
the false lashes, and said she wanted more bass. "Turn
that shit up, Herb," she'd rasp out, as if she'd smoked
two packs of cigarettes a day all her life. If you didn't
know her and only spoke to her on the phone, the deep
voice would make you think she was a man. I helped
record her "KMA (Kiss My Ass) Rhapsody," which became a huge hit at parties, though they wouldn't play it
on some stations. It's in the box with the others. They
all signed their albums for me. So if Chris sells them,

he could probably make a pretty penny. That's one of Eileen's sayings. *So-and-so could make a pretty penny doing this or that.* I used to tease her, "A one-hundred-dollar bill is a lot prettier than a damn penny." I set aside a couple hundred every month for Chris's college fund, pleased to watch it grow.

When he started kindergarten, we bought a three-bedroom place, two doors down from my sisters, and settled in on quiet Maple. Besides Eileen and Chris, my sisters Ella and Doreen were all the close family I had. We lost Pops in a car crash when I was in junior high. And Momma passed when I was in Nam. I found out five weeks after the funeral.

On Saturdays, I sometimes drove around to see if anyone was playing ball, so I could join in, even if I couldn't move the way I used to. Occasionally, a guy I didn't know might ask about the limp. "What happened to your leg, Herb?"

"Got shot," I told him. "Try not to let it happen to you."

On Sunday, Eileen and Chris rode with my sisters to church while I stayed home or hung out with my buddy Les. He was married now too, and his wife visited her folks every Sunday. He didn't accompany her because he had the feeling her brothers and father didn't like him. Les had disappeared from Firenze for a long while, right after graduation. No one knew where he'd gone, although "Canada" got thrown around. He turned back up when the draft ended. "We never should've fought in that war, bro," he said as we sat drinking beers too early in the day. "Wasn't none of our business. How many of us died over there? How many? And for what?" I just nodded.

Most of the time, he talked about his wife Debra. "How can these women change so? She was so shy when I met her, so quiet, and now I can't even say anything in my own house. And the way she dressing these days. Tight clothes, short skirts. You think it's for my benefit, bro? No, it ain't."

Yeah, well, Eileen had changed too. "They're never wrong," I said. "Sometimes it's like talking to a wall. The wall maybe hears what you're saying, but it's not going to change. And if you bang your head against it, you the only one going to get hurt."

Sunday afternoon, when they got back from church, we all piled into my Ford and drove to Aunt Veronica's house, where the usual feast awaited us. Cornbread, greens, pork with barbecue sauce, potato salad, sweet potato pie. Aunt Veronica had learned to make the food her Tommy liked. After we ate, I would take Chris out to play ball in the yard, leaving the women alone. Chris went through the motions, catching and bouncing, though he probably would've been happier sitting in a corner of the den, drawing in one of those sketchbooks Eileen kept buying him. I felt a bit guilty for dragging him outside, but the women's laughter and talk sometimes gave me a headache.

Headaches. Just a little side effect of war. I never wanted to talk about it, as I said. Never told Chris about my time there. And now here I am writing all this down before my brain turns to mush, or soft-boiled rice. Just the thought twists my stomach. Rice. Morning, noon, and night. It's stupid to feel so much hatred for a food, but in the end you can't help it. Eileen loved her rice though. Fried, with beans, with peas, with sardines, with corned beef, with ketchup, with hot pepper sauce. But when she realised I couldn't even watch her and Chris eating it, she cooked it only when I was at work. I usually came home to potatoes and macaroni for the starch. Even grits reminded me too much of rice. Yet, when Eileen got sick and the treatment made her food come back up all the time, I cooked rice for her. It was all she could keep down.

It's funny how you can go along for years, get up in the morning, go to work, come home in the evening, eat, watch TV, never suspecting a thing. You stop eating rice, and all's fine and good. Then out of the blue, you start waking up at night in a sweat, shouting until you're hoarse, frightening the daylights out of your wife and kid. It was always the same dream, and it made me ashamed that I wasn't strong enough to blot it out. I'm a tall man—Chris gets his height from me—and I still had the strong arms and shoulders like when I played ball in high school and that first year of college. But I would wake up yelling, crying, shaking like a little kid.

I'm in the dark, hiding behind a tree. I know I'm surrounded although I can't make out the men approaching. I can only feel their presence, feel them drawing close. I push my body hard against the tree, trying to be one with it, disappear inside it. And all of a sudden they are there, with machetes, and they start chopping, cutting me into pieces. I welcome the blows. This can't go on forever. I know I'm dying, although it's not coming fast enough. Then just as I'm about to lose consciousness, the sun comes out, and I'm still alive, whole. When I look out from behind the tree, I see them, the men who had been hacking at me and then weren't, they're now dragging old men, old women, little children from huts and chopping them like pieces of wood. I start running towards them, as the boom–boom of shots mixes in with the cries. My own screams blast me awake.

The dream started coming more frequently, around October '83, when the military went down to Grenada. In our years of marriage up till then, it was the first time I'd seen Eileen jerked out of her "America is on the whole a good place" attitude. It was now "Your country, Herb." Your country doing this, and your country doing that. Her anger boiled over when she overheard someone at the mall saying, "We goin down there to kick some ass." Oh boy. She didn't find that funny at all, she who had become more American than me. She let loose a stream of patois in the mall, which they probably didn't understand. Lucky for her, maybe. She still hadn't learned not to mess with crackers.

The doctor said it was all the images on TV and in the papers that were making things worse. I asked for pills, but he recommended that I hold off for a while, the damned fool. The sleepless nights were making me irritable and Eileen was suffering too. We were bickering nonstop. And yes, it was mostly my fault. One evening I came home and looked through the refrigerator for something to snack on. But each plastic box contained only the sticky crap. I threw the rice all over the kitchen floor, and I didn't end with that. I cleaned out the refrigerator by throwing every bottle, every vegetable, every carton onto the tiles. At first Eileen tried to stop me. Then she and Chris left me alone, until I got tired and went to bed. The next morning, I found it all cleaned up.

That December, she left for Kaya Bay with Chris for two weeks, saying I needed some space and time to myself. I never told her how much I missed them, how fourteen days seemed like fourteen months.

The doctor recommended a change. Go somewhere else, see new scenery. Some of my friends from high school had already gone north. Les had relocated to Brooklyn the year before. He said there were jobs, that things really were getting better all over the place.

We moved the next year, right around the time that Jesse was running for president. Packed up just three weeks after he visited Firenze and everyone went out to hear him speak, filling all the seats in the auditorium at the university. I knew he didn't have a chance in hell of making it to the White House, but when the basket came around, I dropped in a hundred-dollar bill to help fund his campaign. A lot of people did the same, we all felt so proud he was in the race. He made a pretty penny that evening, as Eileen said. Chris was excited to see him, less excited to be moving and leaving his friends.

"Why do we have to move?" he kept saying. I left it to Eileen to explain that Daddy had a new job. Anansi-man Daddy had to recreate himself, put himself back together.

The change of city lifted my spirits, even if we missed my sisters, Aunt Veronica, and the water around the Shoals. The dreams eased off, and Eileen and I argued less. She was happy she could finally buy some of the food she'd yearned for—patties and roti down on Nostrand—and I liked being able to go for a beer every now and then with Les. Until he got divorced and moved again for good. To Canada.

Chris settled in, and started doing real good with basketball. Over the years, he got better and better, and Eileen and I loved going to the games. I was sure he was going to be drafted by the end of high school. In my mind's eye, I saw him playing on TV, saw him reaching up for a long-distance shot.

But art won.

He and I got into the habit of looking past each other, even when Eileen was sick. But then Lidia came into our lives, with her laughter like sunshine. We couldn't have asked for a better daughter-in-law, Eileen said. More like a daughter even. She helped me sort Eileen's things, two months after we put her in the ground, and I remember when we came upon the box of drawings.

"Wow, look at this," Lidia said, as she leafed through the pictures. Chris had even done a portrait of Jesse Jackson. "These are really good," she enthused. I nodded.

Eileen had kept everything Chris ever did, with

pencil, crayon, pen. I hadn't realised he'd spent so much time on this. Lidia asked if she could have the drawings, and I gave them all to her. I wish I'd kept one.

I wonder where they are now. I would like to ask Chris. But we can't talk about Lidia or anything else. Not yet. His agent Stephen might know though. He called me the other day, just to see how I was. I'm doing fine, I said. Sometimes I forget things, but I'm doing all right. We didn't talk for very long, only a few minutes. I hope he'll call again and let me know when Chris will be back. Not that I'm missing him, but I have the feeling my time is running out.

CHAPTER THREE

They Like the art

"You know, I never had so many visitors in mi life," Miss Della said to Chris one morning as they were having breakfast. She'd made roast breadfruit, plantains, and mackerel, and he felt he was eating in the morning what he should've been having for dinner, but he was getting used to it. He'd just remarked on how nice it was that people kept dropping by to see her, but her burst of laughter made him realise it was his presence that was attracting the visitors.

"Before, people would just shout out hello and go bout their business, cleaning up their house and ting, but now everybody want to come in and waste mi time chatting."

"Sorry," Chris chuckled, surprising himself. He'd thought his laughter had gone for good.

"No, no, don't worry bout it, darling," Miss Della reassured him. "Is not every day they can come see man painting flowers like you. And look how everybody saying how much they like the paintings. We is a nation of art lovers, you know."

She gazed round the walls of the kitchen, at all the paintings he had put up, and murmured, "Dem really do brighten up the place and lift yuh spirit. That's why everybody passing through now, like mi house turn museum. Even Miss Pretty coming in to look. First time she been inside. Although maybe she think is Stephen come back, poor soul."

Chris glanced at his artwork and gave a rueful smile. He still wasn't where he wanted to be. Yes, the things looked more like flowers now, compared with when he'd first got here, but that final aspect, the lightness of touch, was still missing. The stream of people coming by and making their encouraging sounds had spurred him on though. He'd got to know them all. Miss Vera, who was a dressmaker, and lived in the town, although she kept her shell of a house on the hill. She was constantly making jokes, but her eyes held loss, something he recognized. He'd given her a painting on one of her visits, and she'd bustled away so he wouldn't see her crying. Mr. Jordan, the citrus farmer, who he felt sure had a soft spot for Miss Della. Chris teased her about it sometimes. And Miss Pretty, who walked the streets in her faded fur coat, and hardly ever spoke. Her eyes were a muddy river, carrying years of tangled thoughts. Her passage always unsettled him, and set the dogs barking. One day, she had come into the yard, ignoring the animals, and watched him as he painted. Then she had walked into the house uninvited and examined the works on the walls.

"Do you know my son?" she'd asked before leaving,

and he'd shaken his head dumbly. "He's a good artist too," she said, staring at and beyond Chris.

She passed by every day after that, stopping to see what he was doing, the damp-animal odour of the fur coat overwhelming, but she never spoke to him again.

Now he needed a break.

"Miss D, I've been thinking," he said, after swallowing the last piece of breadfruit and taking a sip of the fresh mint tea she'd made, with leaves cut from a robust plant she'd brought up from the nursery.

She smiled at him attentively. He knew she liked it when he called her "Miss D."

"Well, when I was little, I came here with my mother. I guess I was about eleven or twelve, and we spent the whole time in Kaya Bay. I would like to go back there."

He hadn't been anywhere since he'd arrived with his knapsack, except twice to Kingston to buy paint and canvas boards, where he'd found the cost staggering. A trip to the coast would refresh his mind.

"It not too far, you know," Miss Della said. "Depends when you want to go, I might just go with you. I have some cousins up there."

"Mom used to have an uncle who lived there. It would be great to find him, if he's still alive. He used to paint as well. And teach at the high school too, I think. Alton Patterson. That was his name."

Miss Della arranged everything—got in touch with her cousins, acquired the number of his uncle, and secured each of them a room in her cousins' house. In doing all of this, she found out that her relatives were now running a successful bed-and-breakfast, and the idea that they were kind of in the same business made her laugh as she relayed the information to Chris. The final bit of organization was to ask Mr. Jordan to take care of the dogs and to have the only taximan she trusted, Brandon, pick them up on a Friday morning and drive them to Kaya Bay.

Brandon—tall, muscular, with looks and a smile that gave Denzel Washington a run for his money—came to fetch them just after six, when it was already bright outside. Chris helped Miss Della into the front passenger seat, where she could stretch out her legs, before he curved himself into the back. He felt like a boy again, ready to cross the island as he'd done so many years before with his mother.

"We takin the new highway. It much-much quicker," Brandon said as they set off. "Cuts the journey by half. But crazy when it raining."

Chris knew that a foreign company had won the bid to build a massive new highway through the mountains but not everybody was happy with how it had turned out. When Miss Della listened to her radio talk shows, he overheard the complaints about dangerous inclines and assertions that the work had been built with imported convict labour. He didn't know if any of it was true.

The scenery as they ascended from Gap Point made him want to take pictures, but he resisted the impulse, instead mentally storing the images of the azure hills and the low-lying clouds. As they went round the bends, both he and Miss Della couldn't hold back their exclamations at the views that stretched on either side of the highway: trees, green valleys, hills, and more hills. Postcards, all of it. Brandon smiled at their expressions of admiration for the scenery. He kept his eyes on the road, as the highway twisted through the mountains. Still, if his brakes somehow failed on one of the descents, the highway had emergency ramps to the side that would take you upwards, cutting your speed. This was mainly for trucks, Brandon told them.

Before they reached the halfway point, at Unity Valley, the mist came down and all at once they couldn't see anything.

"It happen all the time," Brandon said. "Just out of nowhere like that. Don't worry."

He slowed to a crawl, even as other vehicles on the road sped past him.

"All dem-driver must have superhero vision," Miss Della commented. "Damn set of fools. And when they cause accident is not dem gwine dead, but other people."

After the mist, it started drizzling, but now the hills had given way to the sea, and everything in the distance had different shades of blue—the cobalt water, the lighter sky, and the grey-tinged clouds. Chris leaned his head back and closed his eyes.

He remembered one particular day at the beach with his mother. He'd never seen her so relaxed—her face looking as if she'd shed a mask, her movements free as if she'd discarded a suit of armour. In fact, it was the first time he'd ever seen her in a bathing suit, and she splashed round in the sea with him as if they were the same age, throwing the salty water at each other.

On the beach, later, she bought him a coconut, and as he sucked the water through a straw, he grew puzzled and uncomfortable, not liking the conversation the vendor struck up with his mother.

"So dat is yuh son?" the man asked.

"Hmm mmn," his mother answered.

"And wey him father?"

"In America."

"Ah hope him treating you right?"

"Yes. No problem there," his mother assured the man.

"I don't want nobody takin advantage of you, you know, pretty lady. People tell me seh America no easy."

Chris wasn't quite sure what was going on, but his mother was acting in an annoyingly girlish manner. As he looked at her petite form in the shade of the coconut tree, her skin glowing from their time in the sun, he realised that his mother really was a "pretty lady," as the too-familiar man had said. He wrapped one arm around the coconut, holding it against his chest, and with the other he took his mother's hand.

"Mom, let's go," he urged.

The vendor burst out laughing. "See dat? Yuh son jealous, man."

His mother didn't laugh. Chris gazed into the distance, feeling his skin burn, but he knew his mother was looking at him. After a long moment, he glanced up to catch her smile, and the sweetness made him stand tall and smile back. She said "bye" to the vendor and walked away with Chris to the water's edge, where they sat and drank their coconut water. He didn't really enjoy the taste, but he decided against telling her so.

They were staying at a small hotel, the Kaya Inn, just a five-minute walk from the beach and from her uncle's house. She'd told Chris that Uncle Alton had invited them to stay with him and his wife, but she preferred that they had their own space and could come and go as they liked. She warned him to always say "Uncle" and "Auntie"; no first names here for adults when you were a kid. Not like in Firenze.

He'd met Uncle Alton the day after they arrived on the island, at his rambling house filled with plants, paintings, and way too many chairs, it seemed to Chris. Rocking chairs, high-backed chairs, stools, all in a dark wood and scattered throughout the vast living room and on the verandah. It was as if Uncle Alton were waiting to host a conference or congregation.

Uncle Alton stood medium height—about a head taller than Chris's mother—with a broad open face, short curly black hair, and a ready smile. His wife, Auntie Connie, came from Canada, and had short auburn hair and hazel eyes. She hadn't been able to shed her nasal accent, even when she said things like, "We so glad to see oonu, you know." They had a dog named Lola, which made them much more interesting than Chris would've otherwise found them. He and Lola took to each other right away, and were soon running round the garden.

★ ★ ★

Later, when they got back to Firenze, his mother framed a photo of him and the dog, he holding a stick high and Lola leaping up to snatch it from his hand. A different kind of dog from Miss Della's band.

"We getting close to Kaya Bay," Miss Della said. "Look how the sea nice."

They kept their eyes on the water as Brandon followed the curvy coastal road, and then, between St. Ann's Gap and Kaya Bay, they came upon the accident. Two buses blocked the road, facing in opposite directions with a short distance between them. Cars had stopped and a crowd was on the sidewalk. As Brandon pulled over and they got out of the taxi, they saw it— the body leaning out of one of the buses, the neck with no head.

The people on the sidewalk appeared to be in shock, not knowing what to do. Chris gathered that most of them had been in the buses. "She just feel sick and lean her head out to throw up, and the other bus come down." He looked at the woman who had spoken. She seemed to be in her early thirties, tall and slim with long braids. It was as if she was trying to explain to herself what had happened.

"Poor thing, poor thing," Miss Della said.

Chris felt his stomach churning, and he breathed in deeply to quell the rising nausea. Why did he have to see this? Hadn't he earned the right to some peace? He forced his mind to look at the shapes—of the buses, which had been imported from India, bearing the manufacturer's brand. He examined the solemn people around him—all different heights and levels of roundness. One man was sitting on the ground silently crying. The young woman who had spoken followed his gaze. "Is the driver of the bus that take off her head. He come round the bend too fast. She never have time to pull back inside."

His eyes returned reluctantly to the decapitated figure, and his mind noted the elongation of the bloody neck, framed by the bus window. He felt he knew her. A woman in her sixties, the bile in her stomach increasing with each bend in the road, until she had to lean out the window to vomit, her last thought being of her children, in that second when the other bus roared up.

He knew with certainty that Lidia's final thoughts had been of him and her parents, just as his would've been of her. He walked away from the crowd to where the head lay on the road. Farther along, he saw masses of flowers escaping from a fence, and he strode in their direction. Bougainvillea. Mockingly pink and vibrant in the sunshine. He picked a huge handful of the petals and walked back to the blackened orb on the asphalt. He scattered the flowers gently over the woman's head, feeling the dozens of eyes watching him. Miss Della came over to join him, and they stood there silently for a few moments before returning to where Brandon leaned against a shop wall, inhaling deeply on a cigarette. The police had arrived by then and were ordering the bus drivers to move their vehicles to the side, so the traffic could continue. As Chris trudged back to the car alongside Miss Della and Brandon, he passed the woman with the braids who'd explained what had happened. Their eyes met, and he reached out and gave her arm a comforting squeeze. He noticed the film of tears behind the grateful smile. He knew they would never see each other again, but he would remember her.

In the car, Brandon turned on the radio, and Marley's voice filled the space, asking for the "teachings of His Majesty." They listened to the music, hardly exchanging a word until they reached Kaya Bay.

Chris was still in a sombre mood when he left Miss Della at her cousins' house and went to visit Uncle Alton that evening. He was surprised to find that the old man now lived alone. Somehow he'd been expecting, unreasonably, to see Lola bounding out to meet him and to hear Auntie Connie's nasal greeting. But the only constant was the chairs, still too many of them, on the verandah with the now peeling paint, and in the living room.

"Connie passed two years ago. I sent a letter to your mother . . . I didn't realise . . ." he trailed off, his eyes watery.

Chris wondered if his father had received the notification. He hadn't said anything about it, and anyway, Chris had never envisaged seeing Uncle Alton again.

"I'm sorry about your mother," Uncle Alton said after a pause. "I never expected her to go before me. We all should have kept in better touch, but everybody gets so caught up in the daily grind. I felt something was wrong when the Christmas cards stopped coming." He slapped Chris gently on the back. "It's good to see you, though. Come, let's eat. And tell me about yourself."

Chris followed him into the dining room where a massive portrait of Aunt Connie nearly filled one wall, her bright face and smile welcoming them.

"That took me nearly a year to finish," Uncle Alton said, as Chris looked at the painting before sitting down. "It was hard."

His housekeeper had prepared fried chicken and rice and peas, with slices of tomato and avocado on the side. She came for two hours every day, except Sunday, he said, then she took the bus back home.

"Yes, thank goodness for Miss Sandra. She takes good care of me," he rasped. "You know how old I am now?"

Chris shook his head, not wanting to guess a figure higher than the reality.

"Eighty-one," Uncle Alton laughed. "That's old, right? But I was the youngest in the family—the little brother of your mother's mother. You know what the worst thing about being the youngest is?" He didn't give Chris a chance to reply. "Well, if you're in good health, you just see everybody dying off before you. But I'd hoped Connie would outlast me, even though she was a year older."

Chris nodded sympathetically. He hadn't told the old man anything about his own life and didn't plan to. "What happened to Lola?" he said instead.

"Oh, she lived to a ripe old age, in dog's terms. Fifteen, I think. But she got blind in the last year and it really changed her personality. She became so quiet and withdrawn, not the bouncy Lola you met when you came. We did everything to make her feel comfortable, though. Then one day, somebody who visited left the damn gate open, and she wandered out into the street. She couldn't see the car, of course." Uncle Alton shook his head and sighed.

After dinner, he asked if Chris wanted to see his studio and paintings. The room was in the back of the house, which got the full morning sun, Uncle Alton said. Stacks of canvases leant against the wall and the first impression Chris had was of dozens of women staring at him. Uncle Alton took one up—a portrait of a white-haired woman with wide, bold eyes.

"That's my mother, your great-grandmother," he said as he handed Chris the painting. "Last year, I decided to paint all the women in the family, and anyone who had any kind of impact on my life, and I'm rushing to finish everything before my time comes."

His style was rough, with the features of his subject exaggerated. It was clear he'd relied on his memory and not a photograph. The woman's face had a liveliness as if she were about to tell an amusing anecdote.

"She was full of stories," Uncle Alton said, guessing his thoughts. "And this is your grandmother. One of my two sisters and you mother's mother. As you know, when she drowned, your mother went to America to stay with Veronica, my other sister, after the funeral and everything."

Chris didn't know. He stared at Uncle Alton. "What? She drowned? I thought she'd been ill." He felt stupid for asking.

"Nobody ever told you? Yes, we think she just decided to end it. Just decided to swim away to freedom from the pain, you know. She did it the day after your mother's high-school exams. I guess she wanted to see her through. But she was in such a bad state by then, in so much pain."

"And Mom, how did she deal with it?"

"You must know your mother has always been a practical person. I think she understood. She and I took care of all the arrangements. She cried once—sounds I never want to hear again—and then she was okay. I think."

Uncle Alton gazed at the painting, and Chris examined it too, noting the woman's resemblance to his mother and the dress she was wearing. It was dark green with tiny red poppies that had been painstakingly painted, a contrast with the rough technique elsewhere.

"And what about my mom's dad? Wasn't he around?"

"Oh, him." Uncle Alton burst out laughing, then sighed. "We lost count of the number of women and pickney he had. Somebody said it went up to forty. So, you have a lot of relatives scattered around the island. But he always said your mother was his favourite, until he disappeared when she was about nine or ten. Just went off to England, and if my sister got two letters she got plenty. Remember when you came here as a boy? Well, he had come back from Birmingham, like a lot of these retirees from England coming home now. And somehow he managed to get in touch with your mother. He built a big house in Mandeville. I don't know if you remember that she left you with us one day while she went to see him. He gave her five hundred pounds, she told me, and said the house would be hers when he died. As far as I know, he's still there in Mandeville. Maybe you can visit him?"

Chris didn't know what to reply. His mother had never spoken of her father, and he had no wish to acquire a grandfather, or any other relatives. He breathed in deeply and leant the canvas back against the wall. He'd listened to enough disclosures for the evening. He made as if to leave the studio, but Uncle Alton had picked up another canvas.

"This is your grand-aunt. You must recognize her."

He nodded, smiled briefly. Aunt Veronica in Firenze. With her white husband who had chosen to be black. She had travelled up for his mother's funeral, shaky and frail. He should go and see her at some point, when he got back. And his father's sisters too, Aunt Ella and Aunt Doreen. He wished he'd been better about keeping in touch.

"And this is your mother."

Chris drew in another deep breath as he looked at the old man's rendering of her face. The shining chocolate eyes. The wide yet shy smile. He'd made her teeth too big though.

"Yes," Uncle Alton said. "If I'd had a daughter, I would've wanted her to be just like your mother. How bout you? Any children yet?"

Chris smiled tightly. All at once, he wished he and Lidia had had a child. They'd kept putting it off because he hadn't felt ready. And now he was. "No," he told Uncle Alton. "No kids."

"So, I see you're not in the baby-father business," the old man chuckled. "You need to spend more time down here."

Chris placed the painting of his mother back against the wall. He felt he needed to escape from the studio and the house. But as he turned, he caught sight of a woman with a queenly tilt of her head, holding a red rose in her right hand; he was struck by her intense gaze, as if she could see the future, even as he recognized that Uncle Alton had a definite knack for painting flowers.

"Lady Bustamante," Uncle Alton said.

"Who?" Chris was confused. Was that another family member? Another aunt?

"She was Bustamante's wife—Busta was our first prime minister, but I know you not here for any history lesson. Still, come, let me show you the scrapbook and the photo albums."

Chris felt his head spinning. He sank onto one of the countless chairs in the living room as Uncle Alton went towards the wooden bookshelves that filled a wall, returning with a thick, rectangular, ledger-type book that he dropped onto the dining table. "It was Veronica who started the scrapbook, cutting out pictures and stories from the *Gleaner*. And I inherited the damn thing because it was too much to take to America when she left."

Chris flipped the pages quickly, wanting now to leave and get back to the comfort of Miss Della's laughter.

"Stop! You know who that is, right?"

A tall man in a suit, with a mass of white hair, was dancing with a younger woman who was wearing a gown and, yes, a tiara.

"Bustamante and Princess Margaret, sister of the queen," Uncle Alton proclaimed, as if it were the prize-winning answer to a TV-competition question. "I was there that evening," he muttered, in a softer voice. "I was there."

Chris had to sit for another fifteen minutes, while Uncle Alton sank into nostalgia, relating all the things that Busta and his wife had done for the country both before and after independence; he barely heard most of the information.

At the back of the scrapbook, he saw the clipping about his grandmother's drowning. It wasn't pasted in like the other articles and pictures, just inserted between the final page and the cardboard cover.

"Veronica put that there when she came home for the funeral," Uncle Alton told him.

Chris read it to the last word, without speaking, as Uncle Alton looked over his shoulder. And he thought of sitting beside his mother that day at the beach, drinking coconut water as she stared at the sea.

The telephone rang as Chris was wondering how to take his leave, amidst descriptions of Busta's trade-union battles for workers' rights. The unexpected shrilling dragged Uncle Alton back from the past.

"Who could be calling at this time of evening?" the older man exclaimed. He pushed himself to a standing position, waiting for his joints to adjust before moving to the phone. Chris listened to his sharp exclamations, the "Oh my God" repeated several times, and he wondered what had happened.

"It's Miss Sandra. My helper," Uncle Alton said after he hung up. "Bus accident."

He was shaking. And Chris knew without asking. The head on the road. He stayed another hour to keep the old man company. He wished he'd never returned to Kaya Bay. But perhaps he'd had to be there, just for this: to give comfort when Uncle Alton needed it. Life was just fuckery, he thought. Pure, friggin' fuckery.

CHAPTER FOUR

Hospital Rooms

The day after Brandon picked them up in Kaya Bay and drove them back home—as Chris had begun thinking of Miss Della's house—Stephen called. Chris was outside in the yard at the time, and Miss Della shouted to him to come to the phone.

Stephen went straight to the point: "Chris, sorry, man. Had to take your dad to the hospital. When can you come?"

After he hung up, Chris spent the next two hours calling around before managing to get a flight for the following morning. He was lucky, it was the last seat available, the travel agent informed him, before quoting the astronomical cost. Chris made the booking without hesitation.

He would leave all the paintings, he told Miss Della, and come back for them when he could. Without his knowing it, she told everyone about his impending departure, and that evening they all tramped up to the house to wish him safe travel: Lorraine and Mr. Jordan from the nursery, Miss Vera and the other neighbours who came to care for their empty houses, Miss Pretty in her fur coat. She entered the house for a few minutes, looked at him for a long time, and left without saying anything.

Brandon drove him to the airport at sunrise, along another new road, with the sea on one side and huge boulders on the other. This road used to be flooded during the rainy season, Brandon said, and the government debated whether to build a high wall which some American contractors had proposed. "But the environmentalists got vexed because that would've killed off sea life, you know, something the fool-fool politician-dem never think bout," Brandon chuckled. In the end, they had simply raised the road, an obvious solution to anyone with common sense, Brandon said. And they brought in boulders gained from the excavation for the other highway—the one through the mountains.

Brandon gave Chris a warm hug when he dropped him off in front of the departures area. "Take care, man. Come back and check us."

Chris found he couldn't eat on the flight, although he was already missing Miss Della's breakfasts. But he was pleased he had a window seat. He stared out at the sea and sky for the duration of the trip, without talking to the man sitting next to him. He desired no more words.

Chris knows he will relive this too, over and over in the years to come. Waiting in the hospital room for his father to be wheeled back from the operating block.

The same musty smell of the room, as when he waited for his mother six years earlier. He opens the window. The paint on the outside of the wood is peeling. The pane is single glazing, showing that the place hasn't been renovated in years. Voices of nurses or cleaners reach him from somewhere. He looks outside. They're down below: four women in their scrubs—light blue pants and tops, white coat. One wears a burgundy-coloured uniform. A different department? They sit on concrete steps in the courtyard, next to the garden that this private clinic boasts. It's a pleasant view.

One of the women smokes a cigarette. He tries to listen to their conversation. It's not English, nor Spanish. Polish? He doesn't recognize the language. His father's room is on the third floor, and the trees reach up outside the window. He'd forgotten about the difference in seasons. It's the first of February, and the chill, after the warmth of the island, makes him shiver. But he keeps the window open for a bit longer. Two of the trees sport dried-up brown leaves, waiting for a strong wind to gust them to the ground. But the garden also has firs and shrubbery that provide green among the brown. He knows these details will come back, even when he reaches his father's age.

When you're in a clinic, it's probably a boost to have a room with a garden view. But he can't keep the window open forever. It has obviously been raining, and the cold contains dampness. He doesn't want his father to be chilled when he returns from the operating ward. He tenses as voices sound in the corridor outside. Someone whistles a short tune. The clunk of wheels. A man's cheerful voice says, "304." Not his father then. This is 303. He checks his phone. It's two o'clock. He's been here since eleven fifteen.

Someone knocks at the door. Chris thinks it's perhaps a cleaner, coming to disinfect the room or make the bed in preparation for his father's arrival. A slim man, who's almost as tall as he, with untidy brown hair, enters. His clothes hang loosely on him—black jeans, a white polo, a grey windbreaker. He looks like he's about to go for a game of soccer with his friends. He introduces himself as Dr. Puccini.

"Everything has gone well," he says, as he shakes hands. "He'll be brought back to the room in an hour, but we'd like to keep him here for a couple of days."

Chris nods, thinking that Dr. Puccini looks too boyish to be a surgeon. He must be a couple of years younger at least.

"Tomorrow the nurse will come to take the gauze out of his nose. Until then, he has to breathe like this . . ." He opens his mouth and pulls air in, expelling it loudly.

"Won't that be difficult through the night?" Chris asks.

The doctor gives a half sigh, and a shrug. "It'll be all right."

"And afterwards, will he be able to eat normally?"

"Nothing too hot, or too spicy. Soft-boiled rice."

Chris stiffens. "How about mashed potatoes?"

"That's good too. And he needs to take things easy.

No running around and heavy lifting." He briefly describes the procedure: removing cysts that interfered with his father's breathing, depriving him of oxygen. His father lost consciousness because of this. "It's not an uncommon procedure. Really nothing to worry about. He'll start feeling better soon." Dr. Puccini smiles without showing any teeth, just a slight brightening of the features. He nods and leaves.

Chris watches the door close, then goes to sit in the armchair with the faded grey plastic upholstery and silvery metal legs. The covering is torn on the right armrest, the yellow sponge peeking through. He thinks about all the work, all the materials that go into making a chair like this—aluminium, wood, plastic, sponge. And the thread used to stitch the covering. That's unravelling too.

He stretches out his legs on the matching footstool and slides down in the armchair. He wishes he could sleep. More than anything, he wishes Lidia were here to keep him company. He stares at the high, rectangular clothes closet in front of him. It's a pale shiny blue with a pale grey door. An ugly thing as furniture goes. The colours in the room are grey (chairs, bathroom door, entry door, closet door), white with flecks of brown (the walls), beige (the bed), white (the sheets), light blue (the closet), and black (the small TV screen mounted above the closet). He takes in all the details, seeing the room on a canvas. He misses his sketch pad although he knows he wouldn't have the energy to draw anything.

Despite the window being closed, it's still cold in

the room. The radiator on the wall is way too small to provide adequate warmth. It's an old one with the exposed pipes reaching up and through the ceiling. Everything about the place says pre-1960s. To pass the time, he decides to look up the exact date when the clinic was built, but as he puts the search term into his phone, a message comes in. It's from Féliciane: *So sorry to hear about your dad. How is he? Glad you're back.*

He's doing okay, thanks, he taps in reply. *See you soon.*

The note from Féliciane buoys his mood. He always has the feeling that she's looking out for him, watching his back. She and Lidia had liked each other—two women trying to reconcile their different halves. It created an instant bond.

The next message is from Stephen: *How's it going?*

Good. Thanks, man, he responds. *Call you later.*

He's jerked awake when a pair of nurses wheel his father into the room. Chris stands up awkwardly as they transfer their patient with practised expertise to the bed. "Everything's all right," one says as they leave. He wonders how many times he will hear that.

But his father does seem fine except for the bandages around the middle of his face. Chris touches the older man's forehead, and his father opens his eyes briefly, looks confused, says, "Ah, it's you," and goes back to sleep. As Chris stands by the bed, another nurse enters. She's carrying a bouquet of yellow tulips, which she hands to Chris with a smile.

"I'm sorry," she says. "We don't have any vases."

Chris looks at the tag attached to the flowers, as the nurse checks his father's pulse before going out. *Love, from F. and Leroy.* They're from Féliciane and her boyfriend, whom he has somehow never met. He puts the bouquet on the windowsill and settles back in the chair to wait until the anaesthetics wear off.

Yes, his father will be all right.

part

two

CHAPTER FIVE

Two Fur Coats

Féliciane had just read Chris's message when Leroy entered the apartment carrying something wrapped in plastic. She went over to meet him in the centre of the living room and he kissed her lingeringly, still holding onto the package, which formed a soft bulk between them. He looked pleased with himself. Like a showman, he slowly pulled the garments from the covering and laid them on the sofa. Fur coats. Two of them.

"Oh my God," Féliciane said. "What am I going to do with two fur coats, Leroy? They're fake, right?"

"Wear them. New York cold enough."

"But you know fur is not my thing. People might start coming up to me and offering me money to do you-know-what. One of my friends said that used to happen to her all the time."

So Leroy told her this joke about a woman who was walking proudly down Broadway in her brand-new fur coat when a man ran up to her with a spray can. "Do you know how many animals had to die for you to have this coat?" the man yelled. And the woman turned and said calmly but loud enough for passersby to hear: "Do you know how many nights I spent on my back to have this coat? You better put that fucking spray can away." And the guy was so shocked that he quickly disappeared.

Féliciane didn't find this funny at all. She stared at Leroy as he laughed his head off, wondering how she had ended up with a shopaholic. That was supposed to be *her* domain. But Leroy couldn't pass a store without buying something. All crap, of course, Féliciane thought. Yet, how could you fault a man who constantly brought you presents? And it wasn't as if he was spending her money. Her friend Cecile, for instance—she had a banker husband who took money from their joint account to buy Cecile gifts. And Cecile was always complaining to Féliciane, "If I wanted a gold bracelet, I would've bought the damn thing myself. At least it would be something I could wear. He has horrible taste."

"I totally understand," Féliciane had said during one of their let-off-steam chats. "I guess Leroy likes to spend because he never had that kind of money growing up. You know, he makes better money than a lot of bankers, and if you don't believe me, just try calling a plumber and see how much it costs."

"Tell me about it," Cecile had said, rolling her eyes. "Plumbers are the new bankers."

That's how Féliciane had met Leroy, over a blocked-up toilet. She'd got his number from Stephen, who knew him through somebody else who'd had to summon him during the night to avoid a flooded bathroom. It seemed like everybody up here kept in touch with people they knew from an earlier life. So she'd called Leroy. He came, and she watched him from the doorway as he worked, his movements seemingly efficient. He talked with hardly a pause, asking her where she came from and what she did. He said he'd always liked to draw as a child, but how could you make money doing that? And Féliciane said, "You should ask your friend Stephen. He's the expert. He represents all the artists I know." She didn't tell Leroy about her inheritance, and he still didn't know about it. She told him instead, truthfully, that her parents had bought the apartment for her.

But those fur coats. She'd never worn fur, and every time she saw a woman in one, it made her think of Miss Pretty, the woman on the island that Stephen had told her about, who walked from one place to the next, wearing fur under the blazing sun. He'd told her the story when they'd been close, when he'd let down his guard for a too-brief couple of nights. But that was all water under the bridge. Now he was only her agent, the same as with Chris and the others he represented.

She asked Leroy what she should do with the damn coats, and he answered, "Do whatever you want." She wasn't sure if he really meant it, or if he was hurt or offended, but she decided to go ahead and paint the coats since she had an exhibition coming up in five weeks anyway. She would paint faces on them, a woman with flowing, gold-tinted dreadlocks, the hair streaming behind her as she walked.

Féliciane loved living in New York, feeling this was finally a place she could stay. She'd grown tired of London's gloom soon after she finished her studies, just as she'd been drained by Paris: the rudeness, the aggression, the let's-have-another-demonstration mentality, the I'm-better-than-you philosophy. Her memory of the only exhibition she'd had in her home city still rankled. After a successful run, during which her family and friends had supported her by buying items they'd probably throw away, she'd asked the gallery owner, Bertrand, for the money due her, and he'd paid her a fraction of what she was owed. When she demanded the correct amount, he'd sniffed, "Tu n'es malheureusement pas une artiste qui peut imposer ses conditions." And he'd refused to pay. She'd been shocked at the level of condescension and arrogance, although she'd lived amidst this all her life. She discarded the idea of getting her father involved, as he could've sent a letter threatening legal action, but she knew then that she needed a break from her country.

Still, you can't keep moving. She hoped things would work out so that she and Leroy stayed together, although one could never know. People come, and people go.

The first time Leroy slept at the apartment, he woke her up in the early hours of the morning, saying she was talking in her sleep.

"You kept on saying 'Miss Pretty.' Who's Miss Pretty?"

And Féliciane mumbled, "Ma tante," and kept her eyes closed. He held her and went back to sleep. He didn't understand what she said then, but now he would recognize the words for "My aunt." He'd been learning some French phrases and he yearned to go with her to France. But he was in for a long wait as Féliciane had no desire to go home just yet.

She didn't tell him about Miss Pretty because she would've had to tell him about Stephen, and it might have been hard to explain a connection forged through knowing that you both were essentially the same— terrified of connections. She and Stephen understood each other too well. That was part of why it hadn't worked, would never work. She might eventually tell Leroy, if the need arose. For now she kept thinking of Stephen and Miss Pretty as she painted the fur coats and prepared the other pieces for the exhibition.

Some days she went to the studio to work, although it wasn't the same since Chris had left, even if other artist friends sometimes came in to borrow the space. She hoped Chris had found a measure of healing on the island and had come back in better shape than when he left. She was glad he had returned, even if it was just to care for his father. What had happened to Lidia could've happened to her too, or to any of her friends. Wrong place. Wrong time. You could have a lot of luck or a lack of it. Still, she wished it hadn't been Lidia.

Other times she worked at home, happy to be in the apartment. It had two small bedrooms and a big living-dining area—spacious for New York. She loved the gleaming wooden floors, and the light, especially the light. Since the apartment faced southeast and the buildings across the street were lower, the front room was awash in light from late morning until the sun went down. Féliciane used one of the bedrooms to store her art material and some of Leroy's more outlandish purchases—the djembe drum, the carved Kenyan stool—while a few of her paintings stood on easels in the living room. She knew that her friends wondered how a plumber and an artist could afford to live in such a place, but as Leroy always said, "It's none of their rass business." Several people had tried to pry into their lives, saying things like, "Leroy must be doing very well," but Féliciane would just nod vaguely and leave them to their wonderings. Her motto was: never talk about your inheritance. It was something she'd grown up with—never tell them how you make it. She came from a country where everyone had a hidden stash, or some kind of scam going, some kind of *arnaque*, and it was just something you learned to deal with. As for the inheritance, it had come from her grand-mère, whose father had been a notaire. Her grandmother had left all the grandchildren, Féliciane and her cousins, a tidy sum. Such a legacy was a true gift from the gods when you chose to do art, or when art chose you. Still, the apartment had come relatively cheap because the building across the street was a mafia hangout. They discovered this after her mother and father had signed the papers. When Féliciane paid attention, she could see the men coming in and going out at all hours of the night. It was always better to mind your own business.

Leroy had told her he'd been living in New York for

donkey years. He'd come with his mother when he was fifteen, and while his mother had gone back home years later, he had stayed. Yet, sometimes Féliciane thought he was the newer arrival. He insisted on speaking as if he'd just got off the plane. "Why would I want to talk like them? You think they want to talk like me?" he said, when she asked. She didn't see the point of that attitude, but she only shrugged; whatever made people happy. Leroy's friends told her that she sounded like him when she spoke English, and they found that to be hilarious—a Frenchwoman who had an accent in English like she was born on the island. But she had in fact learned most of her spoken English from the people she hung out with in London, people from the islands, and now Leroy. Her book-English had come from her high school, the Lycée Manislas in the sixth arrondissement where you had to choose what to do with your life three years before you graduated. Everything was set out for you. Féliciane had followed the route and then escaped as fast as she could, first to London to study art and then to New York to do the kind of art she wanted. In between, she'd tried to give her homeland another chance to make her stay, but it hadn't worked.

She knew she appeared as if she might've come from the islands, though, and sometimes she entertained herself by pretending. That was the thing with her kind of skin, you could be from anywhere, and it confused the people she met for the first time. When they asked the inescapable "where are you from" and she responded "France," they looked surprised and gave a long drawn-out *ooohhh*. Sometimes to put them out of their misery, she would add, "My mother is from Côte d'Ivoire and my father is French." Then she could see from their eyes that they were doing the math, blending the hues. People got uncomfortable when they couldn't place you, when you didn't wear the robes they expected you to wear or have the hairstyle or hair texture that provided the much-needed clues.

It was the same with her work. Some people had a problem with installation art, even fellow artists. The thing was—she could paint on a canvas like Monet or Manet if she wanted to, and sometimes she did, but it was the placing of objects to tell a story that excited her, or the images on unusual materials, to catch viewers off guard. Both Chris and Stephen had told her not to listen to anybody, to do what she wanted, even if it was "way out there." She couldn't wait for Chris to return to the studio. Lidia's death had affected everyone in their circle, affected the work, brought out the inner darkness that she was still fighting. Féliciane didn't expect the fake fur coats to create any light, but she had to do something with them. She wondered if she should invite Chris to the exhibition, but then decided against it. Give him time, Stephen had said. She would go to visit him afterwards, when his father was out of the hospital.

The day before the show Leroy came home with two statues of a Rastaman. Not one, but two. *Jamais un sans deux,* Féliciane thought. But it might have been worse. It could've been three. Each statue measured a metre and was carved from a pale wood that looked like pine.

"Where did you get those now? And who's it supposed to be—Bob Marley?"

"A guy from home was selling them on the sidewalk, down on Nostrand," he answered, grinning. "It favour Bob, right?"

"And you couldn't resist? Really?" She didn't know whether to smile or be angry.

"The guy looked kinda hungry. At least now him have some money for food."

A long sigh escaped before Féliciane could stop it. "So where are we going to put them?"

"How bout in front of the window, so that if the mafia people ever start firing shots, we have something to block the bullets?"

She started giggling but then got serious when he looked at her. She remembered how afraid she'd been to go to concerts in the months after killers went on the rampage at home, and this was when she was already far away. Leroy had told her about waking up at night when he was little, with shots exploding all over like in an old cowboy movie, and it even happened during the day too, around his school. She watched him put the statues in front of the window, but far enough back so as not to block the light. He stood still for a moment to take in how they looked, and she walked over and wrapped her arms around his waist from behind. She remembered standing in that same position before, by the window, with Stephen. She blotted out the memory.

"Do you think you could buy two more? Maybe I can put them in the show."

Leroy laughed, turned around, and hugged her.

The fur coats were the centrepiece of the show. Paul, the gallery owner, had invited the press for a preview the day before, and Patricia Merenzo had written in the *Post* that the show was a "bold statement for animal rights." So, earlier in the evening, a bunch of activists had shown up, and everything was going swimmingly until the caterers brought out the foie gras on toast, the little ham sandwiches, and the wild boar terrine. Féliciane had asked the Fondation Française, which was sponsoring the show—her father knew someone who knew someone—to skip the foie gras but she supposed everyone had to do their part to support the local meat industry back home. She heard whispers of "foie gras, can you imagine," "doesn't she know how they force-feed those poor birds," and "what do you expect, she's French, even if she doesn't look it," and the activists marched out.

"I did tell you to serve only ital food, right, Fellie?" Leroy said. "Why you never listen to me?"

But she didn't have time to explain about the Fondation, as Stephen was there now, trying to introduce her to some of the clients he'd brought along. She asked Stephen how Chris was doing, and he muttered, "Fine, fine." Féliciane wasn't sure what that meant, but she had learned not to ask questions. People from the island, and especially Stephen, preferred you to mind your own business, unless they gave you permission to stick your nose in.

She looked over at Paul, whose pleasure permeated the air. He was pasting a red *Sold* dot onto her piece titled *The Lost Sum*. In it she had glued coins she'd found onto a thick slab of wood. The coins had come from all over the city. New York received thousands of tourists who lost their national currency on sidewalks and in parks, and she was always on the lookout when she went walking or jogging. Copper-coloured coins. Silver. Pale gold. Some made of plastic. Bearing the images of kings, queens, long-dead presidents. Paul winked at her and pointed his thumb almost imperceptibly at the installation of rope and tree branches she'd named *Knotted Life*. It looked like that might sell as well. Some people evidently appreciated foie gras. As she gazed at Paul's glowing face, it struck her that he was awaiting the next big thing, the next big artist since his star Cinea Verse, aka Dulcinea Evers, died several years back. But Féliciane knew she wouldn't be The One.

At the end of the evening, the fur coats were still there, and for a moment she and Stephen stood together in front of them, both of them drinking wine from Bordeaux. This was how they'd first met, at an exhibition, he coming to her side as she looked at one of Chris's paintings. But the drink then had been a dark Belgian beer, produced in a monastery for centuries, the label had implied.

"It's Miss Pretty, right?" Stephen asked, staring at the images on the fur.

"Yes. Maybe. I don't know. She's been in my head since you told me about her."

"It is Miss Pretty," he repeated, and she thought of the story he'd told her, during that intense week when he'd slept at the apartment, long before Leroy came to rescue her from a malfunctioning commode.

"Did I tell you she's been demanding to see me?" Stephen asked now.

Féliciane shook her head.

"She got hit by a motorcycle. Some young guy with his new bike. And no insurance, of course. My aunt called me about it. She's lucky she only ended up with a broken leg." He paused. "I might fly home next weekend. Do you want to come with me?"

The question startled her, and she glanced uncomfortably in Leroy's direction. "Stephen, you know I can't."

He too looked over to where Leroy stood, and he gave a slight smile. "Yeah. I understand. Although maybe he could come too? I don't think he's been home for a while." He chuckled drily and turned back to the coats, staring at them as if he wanted to summon Miss Pretty. Then he squeezed Féliciane's shoulder and walked out of the gallery.

Everyone said they "loved" the exhibition, but along with the sense of achievement Féliciane couldn't avoid a lingering dissatisfaction, a familiar sadness. She hadn't yet learned how to manage the guilt. She wanted to tell Leroy about Stephen, and yet there really was nothing to tell. Things happened and you moved on. She wished Stephen knew how to be happy. She wondered, not for the first time, why he hadn't continued to draw, instead of now representing other artists. But she had never seen his work.

She and Leroy strolled home together afterwards, each wearing a fur coat with Miss Pretty's face painted on the back.

CHAPTER SIX

Rememberings

Stephen shoved his hands deep into his pockets as he strode the fifteen minutes back to his apartment, cutting through side streets to avoid the too-bright streetlamps and neon signs of the main roads. Inside the one-bedroom flat, he leaned with his back against the door, taking in the bareness of his living room. A three-seat sofa, a wooden dining table with four matching chairs, a desk and stool. And the massive black-and-white painting Chris had given him, hanging above the sofa, a city at nightfall. The room held no TV, or decorative knickknacks. He liked it this way. Belongings weighed him down, made him stressed.

He straightened, kicked off his shoes, and approached the desk, picking up the notebook with his writings. He'd started jotting things down, the memories from when he went to live with Auntie Della, but nothing from before. He wasn't ready for that.

He thought of writing a letter to Féliciane—he had so much he wanted to tell her. Instead, when he sat down, the words that poured out were about Miss Pretty. He wrote late into the night.

Miss Pretty was crying again today, I told Aunt Della.

Lawd, Miss Pretty always a-cry, Auntie said.

But it wasn't true. She cried only once or twice a month, whenever she stopped in front of one of the houses and saw her reflection in the window. I'd been watching her for years as she strode through the neighbourhood, from the time Auntie took me to live with her. She marched along as if she had business waiting for her, yet we all knew she had nowhere to go and nothing in particular to do. Every Saturday when she climbed up the hill and passed our place, Auntie would put a few things in a paper bag—mangoes, carrots, oranges—and tell me, *Stephen, go give Miss Pretty this*. And I had to race after her, calling out: *Miss Pretty, Miss Pretty, Auntie said to give you this.*

I hated it.

I had to sprint past her, then turn around and face her, to get her to stop. And as I stood there stupidly with the bag in my hand, she drew still on the path, wrapped her fur coat tight around her body, and looked right through me. She always accepted the gift with a, *God bless you, son.*

Why you always have to make me do this? I asked Auntie. And as usual she gave me lectures about "there but for the grace of God go I." I hadn't a clue what that meant, but I felt guilty and ashamed just the same. Sometimes I tried to stay longer at football practise so as not to be there when Miss Pretty passed, but just like spite, she always managed to come down the street, right after I got back. And so it was, *Stephen, mi dear, go give Miss Pretty this for me, no?*

Auntie wasn't the only one who supplied Miss Pretty with a few vittles, vitals, itals, though. As she walked from one end of the neighbourhood to the other, ignoring the dogs barking at her while safely keeping their distance, people hurried to put a little something into a paper or plastic bag and went running behind her fur coat, even in the years of IMF belt-tightening when we hardly had enough for ourselves.

Miss Pretty was probably in her forties, but she still had the lithe body of a teenager, wiry like my aunt who liked to walked too, but only to get from house to nursery to market and back. The coat couldn't hide her leanness nor the long firm legs, and I imagined men in the neighbourhood joking to their wives that they ought to take up walking, and heard in my head the wives kissing their teeth as they slammed something down on the table or stove.

By this time I was now seventeen and getting ready to graduate from high school, and Miss Pretty had walked throughout my childhood. Yet, I'd never said anything to her besides *Good morning*, or *Good afternoon*, or *Here's something from Auntie for you.*

I'd lost count of the stories I'd overheard to explain Miss Pretty's walking, but the one most often repeated was this:

When Miss Pretty was eighteen, her mother took

out a second mortgage, paid a lot of money to get her a visa, and sent her to study art, or something like that, in Canada. Why would anyone want to spend all that money for their pickney to study art? Imagine that, people said. Anyway, while there, Miss Pretty fell in love with a teacher and had his son. The man promised to marry her, but before the wedding could take place, Miss Pretty had an accident. She and her baby's father were going out one night when a drunken driver crashed into their car. On her side. She spent weeks in the hospital, and when she was discharged, she discovered that her baby's father had changed his mind about marriage. *You know how man is*, the women in the neighbourhood said. *You expect little and get less*.

Miss Pretty's visa had run out, though, and soon the immigration people came knocking at her door, in the middle of the night. She had to return to the island, with just the coat on her back, leaving her son with his father who promised to visit but never did. Miss Pretty returned to her mother's house, and people in the neighbourhood tried hard to hide their pity when they saw her broken face, with the deep scars and the mouth twisted permanently to one side. As the years passed, Miss Pretty stopped talking. When her mother died and left the house to her, she started walking . . . in fur coat and turban, paying no attention to the dogs and the stares. People in the neighbourhood said, *Poor thing. She used to be so-o pretty.*

But, you know, in their pity, I thought I heard a kind of satisfaction, and it made me wonder: Was being too pretty a kind of sin? How many had envied her when she was pretty enough to have been a beauty queen? But these were things I couldn't ask Auntie. Instead, I drew pictures of Miss Pretty in my sketchbook, imagining how she was before and erasing the scars she now had. I was never very satisfied with the drawings—I knew I wasn't going to be another Barrington Watson. I would never have been as good as you and Chris if I'd gone into art. But at least they looked a bit like her.

Another version of the story said: Miss Pretty hadn't been to Canada at all. No, once she'd left high school, she'd started working at one of those scandalous hotel complexes farther up on the North Coast, places where the tourists wandered around butt naked as the day they were born, showing all to anyone who wasn't too embarrassed to look. There she fell in love with one of the guests, or vice versa, got pregnant, and found herself fired. The man, meanwhile, had quickly returned to America. Or Canada. Or Germany.

Miss Pretty suffered through seven months of the pregnancy, with her mother at her side. Then, as a taxi was rushing her to hospital for a premature delivery, the driver ran a red light and a minibus slammed into the car. On Miss Pretty's side. The baby was stillborn, and Miss Pretty's face disfigured for life. She started walking when she got out of the hospital.

Our neighbours also said, with that kind of joyless, uncomfortable laughter, you know the kind I mean, that walking was in Miss Pretty's blood, because her father had been a walker too, and perhaps *his* mother as well.

Throughout his life, her father had been one of those who longed to "return to Africa," Auntie told me when I asked about the story. He'd been a tall, good-looking man, with dreadlocks almost down to the middle of his bottom, and he looked more Indian than African. *But who wants to go back to India?* Auntie laughed.

You know, Miss Pretty's mother wasn't into Rastafarianism or dreadlocks at all, Auntie said, *but she went along with that man's foolishness, cooking him ital food without meat or salt, and not saying one bad word bout him to anybody. And she would just look the other way when him roll a big spliff and sit on the verandah blowing smoke up into the air, or when him jump on him motorbike and ride off for yet another meeting with the Sons of Zion.*

From what Auntie and the neighbours said, it was during the seventies, one Saturday night, that Miss Pretty's father got caught in a police roadblock as he was coming back from a meeting. The officers of the law, hating him for his dreadlocks and using the small stash of ganja in his pocket as excuse, clobbered him with their batons and rifle butts, and dragged him to jail, where they shaved off his hair. They kept him locked up for two weeks as a lesson to his Sons of Zion brethren, then they released him. And that's when he started walking, Auntie said. Some people in the neighbourhood joked that if he'd kept it up, he would've walked all the way to Africa, to Zion. But he never got there. A police jeep hit and killed him on the causeway between Kingston and Spanish Town (it's now called the Nelson Mandela Highway) when Pretty was eleven years old.

So everyone agreed that walking was in Miss Pretty's blood and I started thinking that it must be true. The first time I'd noticed her, I had giggled and called out to Auntie, *Look, I am mad like her. Watch me walk.* And I'd marched around the living room, my arms held stiffly at my side, staring straight ahead. But Auntie hadn't laughed. Instead she had run after me, spun me around, and slapped me on the face. *Don't ever let me see you make fun of people like Miss Pretty!* she shouted at me. *You never know what can happen to you in this life!* And when I had stopped bawling like a fool, more from the shock than anything, she gave me a brief, fleeting hug, then a long lecture about illness, how it can attack your body as well as your mind. And if I'd known the words then, I would've told her that I was mocking Miss Pretty to ward off the sense that one day I, too, could end up walking.

Still, Miss Pretty didn't look sick to me at all. In fact, she looked super fit and healthy, only strange and somewhat frightening. I always tried not to look at her face when Auntie sent me to her with the food. I focused only on her eyes—which I could now draw with my own eyes closed—and over the years I began noticing that they grew bright when she looked at me, as if she was starting to see me. Still, I wished that Auntie would take the blasted bag of food herself. I really was getting too big to be doing that now. In a few months, I would be going off to university, yet during the summer holidays before I left, Auntie continued sending me out after the fast-moving back of Miss Pretty. And if I complained about going, she would fix me with a long look that made me think of all the things she had done for me and what a worthless nephew I was. So I would just roll my eyes and stomp out to the path.

One day that July, as I gave Miss Pretty her bag of goodies (that's what I'd begun calling it to my friends), I told her hesitantly, *Sorry, but you won't see me for a while because I'm going to the States to university.*

She stared at me. *Are you going away?* She spoke quite properly, like a schoolteacher, and it surprised me. I found myself stuttering.

Yes, Mam, I'm going to study business in . . . in America.

Her eyes gleamed. *America. Perhaps you will see my son there?*

I started to say, *I thought your son was in Canada*, but different words came out of my mouth without my even realising it. *Yes, I'm sure I'll see him. I'm sure he is fine. He probably looks like you, Miss Pretty.*

Her gaze became more intense, and I couldn't look away. *My name is Cynthia. My name is not Pretty. What is your name?*

My name is Stephen, Miss . . . Cynthia. I held out the bag which I'd almost forgotten, along with the sketchbook containing the drawings I'd done of her. She took them both, and, as the light slowly went out of her eyes, she said, *God bless you, Stephen.*

When I went back into the house, I told Auntie that Miss Pretty had spoken to me. *What she say?* Auntie asked. *Nothing much*, I replied. *She just asked my name.* For some reason, I felt cautious, as if I'd been given a glimpse into a secret world and now had to be careful what I said and did.

The exchange with Miss Pretty was still in my head the following morning, a Sunday, when we heard the commotion in the neighbourhood—a mix of laughter and people shouting. *Miss Pretty, stop, go put your clothes back on!* someone yelled above the babble. Auntie and I went out onto the path to see what the fuss was about, and we stood still and silent at the sight of Miss Pretty marching down in her birthday suit, not a stitch of clothing on, no sign of the fur coat. *Lawd God*, Auntie said. I found myself rooted to the spot, unable to take my eyes off Miss Pretty's bare figure. She had the body of an athlete, like one of the runners I had grown up loving—Junie Johnson. She was firm and brown and toned and more beautiful than I had imagined, and I wanted to continue looking, but Mr. and Mrs. Charles from up the street ran to Miss Pretty with a sheet and forcefully wrapped her in it. I could hear her shouting, *They took my son away! They look my son away from me! I want him back!* I felt an urge both to rush to her and to retreat inside the house, but my feet remained stuck where I was. I watched as the neighbours urged Miss Pretty away, her sheet-robed body disappearing into Miss Vera's house at the top of our street.

Beside me, Auntie shook her head and muttered, *Poor poor Pretty.* She took my arm and we slowly went back to the shade inside the house.

Before I left for university, Auntie sat me down, saying there were things I had to know. But I already knew most of what she had to say, of that story we've carried together all these years. And I've never told anyone. One day, I might tell you, Féliciane.

CHAPTER SEVEN

It's Hot in July for Fur

Most days the sun seemed determined to spite her, to smite her, to push her back to the coolness of her silent house. Before she had taken a dozen steps, she could usually feel the sweat coursing down her forehead, trickling down her back, and creeping between her breasts. She mopped her face with the green-and-white plaid handkerchief she always carried—one that had belonged to her father. She could still picture her mother ironing his handkerchiefs every Sunday evening and folding them into neat squares. He'd had so many, but now there was only this one left and she took it with her every morning and washed it every evening. She hung it on the line in the backyard, beside her turban, the white dress, and the fur coat, and by sunrise the next day everything was dry and ready for the road, thanks to the heat.

When it rained, she had to find another costume and another piece of cloth to wrap around her head, to prevent the sun from frying her brains. Last night it had poured, as if a hurricane was on the way, and her clothes were dripping on the line this morning. She tried to find something else to wear, but nothing was suitable. It was impossible to go walking around in red or sky blue when one was in mourning, and black was suicide in the heat, so white was the only colour that seemed right and correct under her coat. But she hadn't been able to find another white dress this morning, and the coat itself was sodden. She searched the two wardrobes and the chest of drawers, only to find that everything looked and smelled mouldy, with unpleasant furry white spots. She realised that one day she'd have to sort through all the clothes and throw some things away. One day when she had the time to sit down and listen to her own thoughts.

She'd had to abandon the search because the sun was coming up and she needed to be on the road before the heat became too fierce. She forced herself to forget about the dress, about the coat, and it was such a pleasure to feel the air on her bare skin as she stepped out of the house. She inhaled deeply, enjoying the perfume of the morning glory flowers that her mother had planted so many years ago in the front garden. She felt as if she were floating. It took no effort at all to walk up the slope to Victoria Street, and the sun was kind today after the nighttime rain. Its light was gentle as it restrained its violence for now.

She could hear people waking up and moving about in their houses as she passed by on the road. Miss Vera was already out on her verandah when Miss Pretty reached the corner of Victoria Street, but rather than the *Good morning, sweetheart* Miss Vera always gave, Miss Pretty instead heard a strangled *Lawd God have mercy!* As she walked on, she could feel the eyes boring into her exposed back, even as the neighbourhood's brainless, mangy dogs began their irritating cacophony.

Miss Pretty, sweetheart, come back. Don't go walking around like that, she heard Miss Vera yell after her, the woman's urgent voice competing with the dogs' barking.

But she was just hitting her stride now, feeling the blood pumping through her body. *I'll walk until you come back to me, until you're returned to me.* One foot in front of the other. A fast walk, just short of a run.

She was aware of others coming out of their houses, some rushing up to their gates to gaze at her. She saw flashes of male grins and felt the women's frowns. She heard the shouts of, *Go and put some clothes on, Miss Pretty!* She ignored them and kept walking, and was surprised when a man ran up and held her by the arm. Soon a woman joined him and took her other arm, and they both began draping a sheet round her body. As they did so, Miss Pretty heard anguished shouts but didn't realise the words were coming from her own mouth. Then she closed her eyes and said nothing more, allowing herself to be led back up the road to Miss Vera's house. She let Miss Vera take her by the hand and lead her inside.

If you wanted to borrow a frock, why you didn't come and ask me? Miss Vera asked. *You can't go walking around naked as the day you were born, you know. Your mother wouldn't like it, believe me. I can make you any frock you like.*

Miss Pretty didn't answer. She watched as Miss Vera went to her kitchen for a few minutes and came back with a steaming plate of boiled bananas, ackee, and saltfish.

Here, have some breakfast before you start your marathon. The day still young.

Miss Pretty took the plate, and she felt herself smiling as she started to eat. It had been so long since she tasted anything this good, not since her mother passed. When she looked up, she noticed that Miss Vera's eyes were wet.

From somewhere, the memories of Miss Vera and her mother talking came to her. Miss Vera saying, *Everybody like the way you raise Pretty, to have manners and not think she better than anybody else, even though she could be beauty queen if she wanted. She so nice to everybody. Good broughtupsy.*

Miss Pretty put her plate down and got up to leave, the sheet slipping to the floor. *Wait, wait. Don't go nowhere, I soon come back,* Miss Vera said. Miss Pretty breathed deeply and stood motionless while the other woman rushed down her corridor and returned with a short-sleeved white dress that had yellow embroidered flowers around the waistline.

Here, quick, put this on before you go outside again, Miss Vera said.

Miss Pretty stepped into the dress that was yards too big for her and smiled at Miss Vera.

I was making it for one of mi clients, Miss Vera said. *Come, let me zip it up for you.*

Thank you, Miss Vera, Miss Pretty heard herself saying softly, before she walked out the door. As she paused for a second on the verandah, Miss Vera's words floated to her, *Imagine that. Pretty spoke to me!*

Mama never got over my accident. When she saw my face after I got off the plane that brought me back home, she collapsed in sobs right there at Norman Manley International Airport. Lawd Jesus God, look what they do to you over there, *she kept saying.* Look what they do to you. I should've never let you go.

I was a different person when I came back. Take a confident man, remove all his teeth, and make him blind in one eye, and you'll see how quickly his character changes. But thank God I have all my teeth and can see perfectly well. When I look in the mirror, though, I wish I could have my face back.

Miss Vera often sings as she sweeps her verandah, some kind of hymn that goes: I wish I were swimming in the deep blue sea, where the good Lord could rescue me. *I've never heard this song anywhere else, and I wonder if she has made it up. But the tune is so catchy that it stays in my head for the rest of my walk.* I wish I were swimming in the deep blue sea, where the good Lord could rescue me. And serve me tea. And rice and peas. And bring my son back to me.

Miss Vera is one of the few people I sometimes stop to listen to when I'm out walking, minding my own business. Some days her daughter is on the verandah too, looking at me with big, round eyes. But Miss Vera and the boy, Stephen, they never look at me like that. I don't know why I never asked him his name before, although I think he has been running out to give me food since he was knee-high to a cricket, poor soul. Miss Della makes him do it, I'm sure. She's raising him right, just like he's her own. But he would be a good child no matter what, you can see that right away. Decent. There is something special about him.

Yesterday he gave me a book along with the paper bag of oranges and carrots. It was a white-covered sketchbook, which he presented to me with an awkward, shy thrust. I thanked him and hurried home to look at the pages, turning them one after the other in the dimming light. The drawings were all of me, with me in my nice coat, my face the way it used to be. In the last sketch, I wore no clothes, but I had huge splendid wings sticking out from my back, like an archangel. As I stared at the drawing, I felt my heart fly open, and I saw Stephen's bashful face rise in front of me. He's such a handsome boy. And Miss Della raising him right, thank God.

aunties

Stephen relished the feeling of homecoming that began with the plane's descent over the water. The quiet elation intensified when the aircraft cruised to a stop, after landing with one or two bumps on the narrow strip of runway flanked by the sea. As he disembarked and strode across the tarmac, with the waves behind him and the Blue Mountains ahead in the hazy light, he welcomed the heat, the stiff breeze, and the blinding sunlight. No going directly from the plane into a stuffy building today. No, here you got a chance to breathe the ocean air.

He was glad that the government hadn't moved the airport inland, to protect it from hurricanes and flooding, as the politicians had discussed. This was where it belonged, and nothing should be changed. He remembered Aunt Della taking him to the airport when he was a child and both of them going up to the gallery to wave farewell to some cousin or aunt of hers, heading to England or America. Back then people dressed up to travel. He smiled as he thought of himself and his fellow passengers—tee-shirts, shorts, sandals, sneakers. One guy was even wearing flip-flops with socks.

He strode through the long humid corridor, and felt the sweat trickling between his shoulder blades, down his back. It didn't take long for his clothes to begin sticking to his body, but fortunately the air was cooler in the immigration hall. A woman dressed in the usual official blue uniform showed him to a machine that scanned his passport. This was new; it hadn't been there the last time he came home. The woman smiled at him as he passed through successfully, and he smiled back, as if they'd just triumphed over adversity together. Then he was in the crowded baggage area, waiting for the two suitcases stuffed with the presents Aunt Della had instructed him to buy: fabric for Miss Vera, bangles for Lorraine, two duckbill caps for Mr. Jordan to protect him from the sun, plus seeds for his farm, and a new fake-fur coat for Miss Pretty. Something lighter, less hot. Thank goodness Féliciane had agreed to help him shop, with her "no, not that" full of authority to which he deferred.

He scanned the lines to see which customs officer might be the least likely to give him hassle and settled on an older, greying man, who was waving other arrivals through in a bored fashion. When it was Stephen's turn, however, some unidentifiable thing caused the man to perk up, as if the hour for his daily dose of fun had arrived. *Do I look like a blasted drug dealer or something?* Stephen wondered, after the man had him heft his suitcases onto the counter.

"Any electronics? Computer equipment? Mobile phone?" the man demanded, removing items from the first bag.

"Yes, just a smartphone for my aunt. It's a gift."

The man paused, his eyebrows arched. "Her birthday? Early Christmas present?"

"No, just a surprise because I haven't been home in a while."

"You have the receipt? We have to calculate the amount of duty you need to pay."

Shit, Stephen thought. He smiled at the man and adjusted his accent. "I think I have it somewhere. I just bought the phone because my auntie getting old, you see. I don't know how much longer she have, and I want to teach her an easy way to stay in touch with her grandchildren."

The man's eyes softened, and his lips couldn't fight the smile. "My daughter bought me one last year too. She live in Canada. Can't believe some of the things you can do with a phone these days. And my wife is so happy to see the grandpickney when we talk to them."

He helped Stephen to put his belongings back into the suitcase. The fur coat took up one whole side of the first bag.

"This coat for your auntie too?" the man asked.

"No, for another auntie," Stephen grinned. "You know, you can't give a present to one without something for everybody in the family."

The man gave a brief, dry chuckle. "I hope she not planning to wear it in this heat. Enjoy your visit home."

Stephen breathed deeply as he walked away, wondering how the woman waiting next in line would fare. She had two humongous suitcases, in addition to her oversized handbag—a fake Louis Vuitton, but then again, it might be real. He had seen her at the check-in counter in New York too, and overheard a staffer telling her in a resigned voice, "Your bags are overweight." And the woman, equally resigned, had pulled out her purse without complaint, to pay the additional cost. He hoped that what she carried was worth the extra riches to the airline and that the man would go easy on her, whatever story she invented. Perhaps she had lots of aunties too. Relatives who needed shiny American electronic goods. He wondered if customs officers had a quota: catch at least one culprit per flight.

He gazed around as he exited the low-ceilinged building, back out in the heat and glare. Shaking his head no to the surreptitious queries of "Taxi?" he headed toward the street. Aunt Della had told him she was sending someone to pick him up and given him directives on what kind of vehicle to expect. As he got to the curb, a gleaming olive-green SUV pulled up in front of him. The driver rolled down the window and grinned.

"Stephen?"

"Yes. Brandon?"

Brandon laughed and leapt from the vehicle. "You just come out?"

"Yeah. Just now. Perfect timing, man."

"Well, I thought that by the time they search you and everything, you would be out around now. You have to pay any fines? You bring new TV for yuh auntie?"

Stephen laughed, liking Brandon right away. He thought that after seeing Miss Pretty and dealing with his aunt's business—Chris had told him about the leaking roof—he would have Brandon take him to galleries around the city, and maybe in MoBay, where tourist demand had created some kind of an art boom. He never actively sought out "new talent," to use Paul's words; clients usually came to him. But it wouldn't hurt to have a look at the market.

The drive to Port Segovia took more than two hours, as they cut from south to north across the island, winding through the hills. Brandon chattered as if they'd known each other for ages but he didn't take his eyes off the road.

"My aunt said you're a good driver," Stephen commented.

"Well, after the accident we see last month . . ." He tailed off.

Later, when other drivers sped past, their aggression filling the hot air outside as they glanced at him with blistering scorn for his pace, he said to Stephen, "Let me know if you want me to go a bit faster."

"No, this is fine," Stephen assured him. "Maybe all those other drivers have pot cooking on the fire."

Brandon burst out laughing. "You sound just like yuh auntie. Too many mad people pon the road on dis-ya island. You know, she wanted to come wid me to pick you up, but then she realise she wouldn't have enough time to prepare yuh feast."

Stephen's phone rang fifteen minutes into the drive. "Everything all right? Brandon pick you up? Tell him not to drive too fast."

"Yes, Auntie. On the way. Everything's fine."

They reached the house in the late afternoon, and Aunt Della came out to the path as he stepped from the car, surrounded by her yapping, gyrating dogs. He hugged her and she hugged him back. This too was new. When he was growing up, they'd always been reserved about showing open affection with each other. She hadn't been the hugging kind and neither had he, although he remembered her holding him tightly as he got ready to board the plane off the island when he left that first time to study.

Caught up in the moment, Aunt Della hugged Brandon too. "Thanks for bringing him home in one piece," she laughed.

"No problem, Auntie," Brandon beamed.

So, he was calling her Auntie too? Stephen was amused. He wondered what Chris had ended up calling her.

Brandon helped him to carry in his bags, and they stood for a moment in the kitchen as Aunt Della bustled around. Food for a battalion covered the table, and Stephen suddenly felt like the prodigal son, waiting for the neighbours to come to his redemption feast. Normally, some of the them would have been there to welcome him, but he now knew about the empty houses and the landslide that his aunt had kept secret.

"Pretty is upstairs," Aunt Della said, when Brandon had gone.

"What?"

"She staying with me until she get better because she can't really move around for the moment. When she came out of the hospital, me and Brandon and Mr. Jordan had to carry her upstairs to the bedroom."

"Oh. Does she realise I'm here now?"

"I didn't tell her. You know, she convinced you is her long-lost son. So just pretend."

"What?" Stephen felt stupid. "You want me to pretend to be her son? So, I should call her Mom or something?"

"You don't have to go that far. Just nod to whatever she say."

Why did Aunt Della always put him in these situations? Of course, he'd always felt a bond with Miss Pretty, but it had nothing to do with blood ties, only mental ones. He'd felt her depression as he knew his. But so far he'd managed to keep from the edge, from walking the streets.

"I'll go up and say hello before we eat. So, she's talking now?"

"Yes, since the accident, look like she find back her tongue. Bruk her leg, get her voice. You can take her up some food."

She heaped rice and peas, chicken drumsticks, and avocado slices on a plate, while Stephen washed his hands at the kitchen sink. Travelling always made him feel grimy.

He looked around at Chris's artwork and thought, *Not bad at all.*

"You see how much painting him do?" Aunt Della said. "I hope him coming back for some of them."

"Yes, he's planning to, and I think I'll take a couple back with me, if you don't mind."

"Take as many as you want," she laughed.

He watched as she took a pitcher from the fridge and poured a clear liquid into two tall glasses. It was coconut water, which would help with Miss Pretty's healing, she said. She handed him the second glass and he drank thirstily. It was all the rage now, she told him— people drinking coconut water left, right, and centre because suddenly the world had woken up to its health benefits. He told her he'd seen shelves filled with cartons of the beverage in New York, sometimes mixed with orange or pineapple juice. He'd tried one of the brands once and hadn't been able to swallow more than two sips. The slightly rancid taste was so different from the real thing.

He put a knife, fork, and napkin into one of his pockets, and took his time going up the stairs, balancing the full plate and the glass. On each side of the stairwell hung canvases Chris had painted, and he used this as an excuse to go even more slowly, stopping to look at the flowers. He was apprehensive about what to say to Miss Pretty, what she would say to him. He rapped with his elbow, and when no answer came, he eased open the door. She was lying on the right side of the bed, with her eyes closed. The rays of the late-afternoon sun bathed the room in amber, and the first thing that surprised him was her hair. The long dreadlocks—which he'd seen in their full glory only once before, when she walked naked—had turned white as clouds, spread out against the navy-blue pillowcase. Her face in repose was less twisted than he remembered. He stood looking at her, holding the food. Her eyelids flickered, then she seemed wide awake, staring at him.

"Hello, Miss Pre . . . Miss Cynthia." Just in time, he remembered the name she'd told him so many years ago.

"Stephen," she said clearly, as if she'd expected this. "You're home."

He put the plate and glass on the night table and helped her to sit up. He handed her the cutlery and smiled at her. As Aunt Della had requested, he slipped into the role of son, to this madwoman from the street.

His father's family had insisted that it was insanity. Before Stephen left for university, he'd read all the newspaper clippings that Miss Della had kept on the case, all the articles that had brought her to the orphanage to get him. It could only be madness that had caused his father to do what he did, the family said. He had always been a little peculiar. But the police force had accepted him into their ranks and everyone thought that meant he was normal.

Stephen didn't remember much from his early years, but that day lived clear in his mind: how he had waited at school for his mother to get him until a neighbour came to collect him from the headmistress's office, three hours after classes ended; how he shivered from a sudden chill when the neighbour took his hand. Later, he would wonder if his father would've killed him too if he'd been home. Then followed the thought that if he'd been there he would have been able to save his mother. He remembered sitting in the front row at Holy Trinity, watching everyone cry, while his own eyes stayed dry in his feverish face. He didn't go to his father's service. Nobody took him. And when his father's sister came for him at the neighbours' place and informed him that he was to come and live with her, he put some crackers and an orange in a bag and slipped out when no one was looking. First he ran, and then walked until he couldn't anymore. He ended up in Maxwell Park and spent six days there, sleeping on the benches, begging for food, peeing and shitting behind the bushes in the park, and wiping his behind with leaves. He noticed that he was beginning to smell.

It was the director of Anfields Children's Home herself who found him there and took him to the orphanage. Mrs. Bennett, whom the children called Auntie Myriam. Through his mumbled answers, she deduced who he was. He'd been reported missing and people had searched for him, thinking he was a casualty in a larger crime—not just a simple thing of a man killing a woman because of jealousy, thinking that she had a lover and that people were laughing at him behind his back.

The *Star* rushed out Stephen's story when he was found, his picture on the front page—a boy whose father had killed his mother. Shot her five times with his policeman's pistol, then put the gun to his own temple. Aunt Della had seen the coverage. But obviously not Miss Pretty.

"My son, I knew you would come back," Miss Pretty said, eyes alight. He hoped it was a generic use of *son,* but he thought not.

"Yes. I'm going to stay until you're better. Until you can walk well again."

Miss Pretty chortled. "That might take months, my love."

He didn't tell her he had a maximum three weeks at "home."

Aunt Della accompanied him the next day to look at the empty houses, and the neighbours' faces swam into his mind. The street felt such a different place now. Later she took him down the hill to the new homes and to the nursery, and he handed out presents as if he were Santa Claus. He'd last seen them seven years before the landslide—he couldn't say why he hadn't been home before; the time flew and months turned into years— and now everyone wanted him to listen to their stories. They sat on Miss Vera's verandah where she poured him and Aunt Della lemonade and spoke of her daughter Teena who lived in the States, like him. Miami though. Did he remember her? They used to be friends, sort of. Teena knew how to speak Spanish now. Miss Vera didn't mention her husband, but Aunt Della had already filled him in. Gone off with a younger woman. Twenty-four years old. Can you imagine? He could. But he didn't say so.

"That's why I so lucky I never married anybody," Aunt Della said. "Better off being on your own." She had glanced at Stephen apologetically afterwards, to show she hadn't been referring to his mother and father. But he knew she hadn't, and he believed in the truth of her words. Better to live alone.

Aunt Della had tried to explain his father's actions to him. Temporary insanity. Crazy jealousy. It happens to everybody, especially men. Women usually just burn the man's clothes or cut his belongings to pieces. Sometimes they find the sweetheart and slap her around. And a few might try to poison the man, mix in a little something with his food. But they don't run for guns and knives. She didn't know why men behaved like that. Maybe because they think they own women. But not all men are the same. "You should know this, Stephen, even if I personally choose not to have anyone in mi life. Well, except for you, dahlin. Always remember that it wasn't your fault what happen. Never ever think it was your fault, you hear me?"

But those were just words. For years, he'd privately sketched images of his mother, father, and himself, in different settings. At Hellshire Beach, at the movies, at Hope Gardens with clouds of bougainvillea in the background. He never showed them to anyone and tore them all up before he went away to college. There he set his mind to his business studies and banished thoughts of drawing. He'd never really been good at it, anyway. The last drawing he'd done, he'd given to Miss Pretty, and she'd probably torn it up too.

It was Aunt Della who had suggested he go abroad to study. Maybe she'd sensed him slipping downwards, although he was sure he hid it well. She had enough saved up, she told him. Go. And he'd gone, thinking he'd be back to live with her again after his degree. But with a scholarship for an MBA, then a job offer at a museum, and the string of short relationships—home became somewhere else. He'd sent presents, spoken on the phone, and returned only twice for short stays. Aunt Della had never criticised him for his absence, though, she'd simply acquired a couple of dogs. For protection, she told him.

By his second week, Miss Pretty was hobbling around and chafing to start walking again. She tried on the coat he'd brought and asked him how she looked, and he said, "Beautiful." He'd almost added "Momma," but Aunt Della had told him not to go too far. He'd got so much into the role, however, that it was hard to snap out of it now. He needed to leave the house more. It was starting to feel like an asylum.

One morning, after taking Miss Pretty her breakfast, he headed to Kingston with Brandon, determined to see some art, as he'd planned. He started with the National Gallery, rushing to look at the paintings by Cinea Verse that Paul had described. Cinea had "taken her leave," as Paul termed it, by the time Stephen met him, but Paul kept building her legend as the greatest artist the island had produced. As a consequence of all the hype, these paintings Stephen now viewed were worth thousands.

And not in local currency, where "thousands" now meant a bag of groceries at Monarch's.

More of the paintings existed, too, hanging in private collections and official buildings. Cinea's best friend, Cheryl McKnight, had started a gallery devoted to her work, with temporary exhibitions every so often of other artists. He visited that next, asking Brandon to come back in a couple of hours after dropping him off. The gallery was on Sheffield Drive, near Anfields Children's Home—the place where he'd become a nephew.

Cheryl wasn't there, and instead he discovered tall, flirtatious Jasmine Wong, whose oversized paintings were currently on show. Wearing a light yellow sleeveless dress that showed off her toned arms, her dyed fuchsia hair in bantu knots, Jasmine greeted him warmly and explained that she'd been given the job of manning the gallery in Cheryl's absence.

"Cheryl is on her honeymoon in the Bahamas," she informed him. "Finally got married after years of putting things off. Do you know her personally?" She gave him a suggestive look, as if expecting him to be deeply disappointed by the information.

"Oh. Good luck to her," Stephen said, trying to suppress the pessimism he always felt on news of marriage. "No, we haven't met. She's a friend of a client. Why did she keep postponing her wedding?"

"Well, things just kept happening, it seemed. First her aunt was diagnosed with a brain tumour, then her cousin, the aunt's son, had a nervous breakdown, and on and on. The time just never seemed right. Luckily, she has a patient man."

"How are the relatives now?"

"Sad to say, the aunt died," Jasmine told him. "But her cousin Trevor is recovering. He's really such a nice man. Always so concerned about everything, taking on the politicians and warning us about global warming. He used to be on the radio all the time."

"Hmmm, that's interesting." Stephen was getting a bit tired of the chatter. He wanted to take a closer look at the paintings.

"What about you? You married?" Jasmine asked.

"Me? No. Do I look married?"

"Do married people have a certain look?"

"Yes. Burdened."

She laughed. "Remind me not to propose to you."

She took him round the gallery, explaining her work. The semi-abstract paintings all had to do with her transition, from Jason to Jasmine. Blue streaks turning into pink roses. Thick lines becoming intricate circles. Stephen was impressed that she was brave enough to put it out into the open, on canvas, on the island. But he knew things were changing, the prime minister had said so. He'd read that in a *Times* article after the man had given a speech at the UN in New York. *No one is giving us credit for the changes,* the PM had complained.

"Do people ever . . . do you ever have any trouble?" Stephen asked.

She smiled, a curl of the lips. "All the time."

He invited her to lunch and helped her to lock up

the gallery before they walked down the road to Carib Grill, where the illustrated menu showed all the basics in heightened, appetizing colour. Jasmine said she was vegetarian, so they ordered rice and peas, callaloo, and plantains, with fruit punch that was like nectar.

"Nothing like a sugar shot," she commented.

"Yes. Sugar, water, and a bit of juice. Just the way we like it."

Over lunch, she told him she was looking for a place to stay as her landlord had asked her to leave, claiming he needed her apartment for one of his children. She suspected that the other people in the building wanted her out, despite their smiles and their congratulations on how good she looked, but she didn't want to get into any cuss-cuss with the landlord or the neighbours. She preferred to leave and shake the dust of the past off her feet.

"It's their problem if they can't deal with you," Stephen said. "Not yours."

"It's mine if I can't find a place to live," she retorted.

"But, if I may ask, why do you feel the need to put your business out there in your art? Isn't it better to just keep things private?"

She didn't appear angered by the question. "It's who I am. Why should I have to hide?" After a pause, she continued: "I've never been fully anything, you know. Half Chinee, half black. Half boy, half girl. Half painter, half singer . . . yes, I have two CDs that I can sell you if you like jazz. Now, I've decided to be fully me."

"There's nothing wrong with being more than one

person," Stephen said. "You wouldn't believe how many roles I'm playing right now."

"Do tell."

But he decided to change the subject, the practical part of his mind in gear. *Find a way,* Aunt Della always said. "Look, maybe you could take my room at my aunt's place after I leave, if you don't mind living in the so-called country. I mean, it's not that far, and she's had an artist staying there before. Do you want me to ask her?"

"Yes, please." Jasmine sounded hopeful and doubtful at the same time. "It would be just until I can find something else here, and it would give me time to work on the next show."

"If she says yes, I'll leave it up to you to tell her what you want."

"Sure, no problem."

"But I want something in return."

"You want me to marry you?"

"Good one. But I'm not the marrying type. And besides, I think I already have a girlfriend. No, first I need to ask you to help out with my . . . mother. Her leg got broken in an accident, and she's staying with my aunt for a while."

"Oh, sorry to hear that. Okaaay. And what else?"

"And I want to represent you in the States. Make some money for you to pay my aunt a good rent."

She hooted, and he laughed along.

"So, what does your girlfriend do?" she inquired as they left the restaurant.

"Oh, she's an artist like you. Installations though. She's French."

"Ooh la la," Jasmine mocked. He smiled at her, wondering if he should add that his "girlfriend" lived with someone else and that his "mother" and aunt were . . . He didn't know where to begin.

He accompanied her back to the gallery, then strolled down Sheffield Drive, in the direction of Anfields. It looked the same—except for the fresh coat of cream paint and the missing naseberry tree in the front yard—a big, colonial-style house of nine rooms where a woman had taken in lost children and tried to find them guardians. He stood in the shade on the other side of the street for a few minutes, gazing at the house. There was no point knocking at the gate. He knew that Myriam Bennett was no longer inside. She had acknowledged his gifts to the home right up to the end, first sending handwritten thank-you notes to his postal address in New York and then emails, which she signed *Auntie Myriam*. In his most morbid moments, he sometimes thought: lose a mother, gain a million aunties. It sounded Confucian. When she died, the government had taken over.

Brandon was keen to take him to other galleries in the city, but Stephen felt drained, by the heat and his memories. They arranged instead to travel to MoBay the following weekend, and en route they would take a short detour to Kaya Bay because Stephen wanted to see the artwork by Alton Patterson that Chris had described.

Who knew how much longer the old man might have? He needed an agent while he could still paint.

When he got home, Aunt Della welcomed the news that she might soon have another artist-boarder. She told Stephen that she'd really missed Chris when he left because the house felt so empty. Then Miss Pretty had her accident and it seemed only natural to take her in.

"It will be nice to have somebody else here when you go back to America," Aunt Della said. "In fact, you know, I was thinking this could be kind of a long-term thing."

"What do you mean, Auntie?" Stephen asked.

"One of these residence-type things I hear bout. Have artists come and stay. They popping up all over the north coast." She went to get the phone he'd given her and patiently taught her how to use that first week. "Look at this one. I screen-shot it."

Stephen stared at her in amazement.

"Some little old house," she said. "We have a lot more room, and I bet I cook better too. What you think?"

"That is a great idea, Auntie," Stephen answered slowly. "A really great idea."

CHAPTER NINE

Uncle Alton and the B's

I could've done without seeing anyone just now. But when he called up and told me he's a friend of Chris's, I said, Okay, come and visit if you wish. And it seemed that he arrived right after I hung up the phone, so quick was he here in Kaya Bay. I was expecting someone as tall and muscular as Chris, but this Stephen is a slightly built man, like a long-distance runner, and he has a quiet way of talking. His eyes are direct, and he gives the impression that if he says something he'll do it. Good manners, even if the bottom line might be money. I like that he's not flashy. Some of these young people who've lived abroad come back dressed as if they've just stepped out of an American movie. There's a sober air about him, a seriousness, maybe even some kind of sadness. Still, who knows what motivates people these days? When I used to teach, I could sometimes pick out the students who'd lost a parent, who went home to an empty house while their mother worked, who came to school with a hungry belly. Now, I'm not sure of anything, except that life is always ready to give you a good kick.

Did I want an agent? he asked, after I showed him the canvases. I could only laugh.

I replied, I'm over eighty. I'll soon be gone. What do I need an agent for?

To sell your paintings, he said. What are you going to do with all of them otherwise?

Leave them for Chris, I said. It was his turn to laugh.

Chris has enough of his own work to store, he said. He wouldn't have the space.

Well, I've already willed the house to him, so he could turn the place into a gallery or something, I said. Anyway, please don't tell him about the will yet. Everything in good time.

He nodded. He was quiet for a while, drinking the orange juice I'd poured him. I felt a bit bad for being so uninterested in his proposal, but since Miss Sandra was taken in that ungodly manner, I find that I don't care about much anymore. Another one gone before me. Soon it will be my turn. I couldn't even do a painting of her, although I wanted to, as a present for her children. But the whole head thing just kept me back. I couldn't stop seeing her head as separate from her body, gone its own way.

She had a closed casket at the funeral, poor thing. Chris stayed on an extra week for the service, then went back to Port Segovia with his landlady. Miss Della, who Stephen tells me is his aunt. She came to the service too. A nice woman. Maybe I'll paint her one day. But what am I talking about? I don't have many days left. I wasn't aware I'd said this aloud until Stephen nodded, agreeing with me.

That's why you should let me represent you, he said.

I sighed. I feel so tired these days. So tired. When I was in my seventies, I was still running around, full of vip and vam. Now I just want to rest. I miss Connie. I miss Eileen. I miss Miss Sandra. And I don't know how to have her stop appearing headless in my dreams. Maybe she really wants me to do a painting of her with her head reattached. Connie was good at telling me what my dreams meant.

Stephen asked what I would do if I had extra income. Then he rephrased the question: what would you still like to do with the years you have left? I chuckled because he reminded me of that Billy Graham preacher man. We used to get his services on the radio long ago, direct from Minneapolis, Minnesota. Many apples, many sodas, the people round here used to say. Or was it Oral Roberts who was on the radio? Both had equally annoying voices, talking through their noses.

I guess I would travel, I told him. Go to all the museums with all the art I would like to see—the Louvre, the Prado, that one in Austria with the Brueghels. Maybe go to Senegal and see the new museum of African civilizations. Have you been to Africa? I asked him. He hadn't.

Me too, he said. One day I'm going to travel around the world. But you need cash for that. I don't suppose your pension is that big?

No, I was a teacher. We're at the bottom of the pile. But I get by. I managed to support myself and my wife quite well. She was a teacher too for a while, came down from Canada on a short-term contract. After we married we never had any real financial problems. Out here in the country, there's not that much to spend your money on.

He wanted to see the early paintings again, the ones I did when I was in my twenties and thirties, about Independence and such. He seems more interested in these than in the portraits of the lovely women in my family, I don't know why. But I guess he's an expert on what might sell abroad. Not that I have any intention of selling anything. He took up the one of Lady Busta-mante and asked why I had painted her, so I told him the story. Stephen seemed to listen a bit more attentive-ly than Chris, who hadn't really been that interested, I could see. But Chris wasn't born here, so he has other stories that are probably more important. Stephen said he first went away when he was seventeen, and it's funny because I went abroad too, but when I was nineteen. I went to America to study and became so distressed by how they treated black people, I couldn't wait to come home. I was twenty-four when I came back with my degree and got caught up in Independence fever. You never saw people so happy—it was like everybody was drunk on white rum. And Busta was there, leading us all on, helped by Lady B., who wasn't his wife yet.

His was one of the first portraits I did, I told Ste-phen as I handed him another canvas. He held it out in front of him as if he was already seeing it on the wall of some museum, or in the house of some collector, but that one is definitely not for sale.

My aunt used to talk about Busta, Stephen said. I know who he is.

Well, I knew him. Him and his beautiful wife. A wonderful woman. So kind. So full of energy to change things for the better. I used to call her Aunt Gladys when we worked together. Seems like most people have forgotten about Busta already, though, forgotten about how they put him in jail for trying to get workers better pay. Look at the party he created. It doesn't have a thing to do with workers these days, all them lawyers now running things. People with money in their pockets. Which one of them is working class?

I couldn't tell Stephen all I wanted to because he didn't have a week to stand there listening to me rant-ing, but memories raced through my head, just as when Chris visited. Different memories this time. I was so full of anger when I came back home, knowing how little people thought I was worth because of my colour. But if things were hell in the States, they weren't that much better at home. Busta was showing us we didn't have to just sit and take it though.

He was seventy-eight when he became our first prime minister, did you know that?

Really. So old? Stephen asked. He looks younger in the painting.

I nodded. I had done two paintings of Busta and given one to him and Lady B. In the one I gave him, he looked even younger. I always felt there was no point in making people feel unhappy about how they were portrayed. Just call me old-fashioned. He loved the painting, kept it in their living room the whole time.

How did you start working with them? Stephen asked.

Well, when I got back from the States, I wrote to Busta. They weren't married yet. She was his secretary at the time, and she was the one who wrote back to me, the one who interviewed me. We clicked right away, like an aunt and her favourite nephew. She must have been fifty at the time, twice my age, and she had come from nothing and built herself up, put herself through school, learning secretarial skills. She was interested in education and she and Busta gave me the job of going round and visiting people in their yards, all over the city, giving out milk powder and biscuits if they needed food, and asking them if they were sending their children to school. All three of us were country people but we had ended up in Kingston because that's where the work was. The yards shocked us, though, people living on top of one another, in dark little rooms.

I wanted to tell Stephen about all the riots that had happened in the year I was born, things my father had told me about, and how Busta stood up for people, but I could see his eyes glazing over. People have no patience these days. And the last thing they want is stories from old people. So I just said: I met them at the beginning of '62, to cut a long story short.

Wow, Stephen said. So you were there at Independence?

His voice held awe, making me feel ancient. Your aunt must have been too, I said. But she might have been a teenager. I was a young man raring to help build our new land.

I laughed when I said that. I don't know what we've built, but I tried to do my part, going back to the country and teaching art and math, helping my mother and sisters when my father passed and we all moved here to Kaya Bay. I've seen so many people leave, so many people pass on. And now here I am with just the paintings left.

Stephen was looking at the one of Lady B. again. I'd tried to capture her sweet smile, along with the regal look.

But Independence. We had parties for days. Lady B. got me an invitation to the official ball, and I was there that night, sitting close to her when Busta twirled round the dance floor with Princess Margaret. The queen had sent her flighty sister. The one who loved a good time. It was just as well. Everybody liked her. At one point that night, Busta introduced me to her and she said: You must come to England and visit us. And she said it as if she meant it. A whole lot of other people accepted that invitation. But not me. There was nothing drawing me to the mother country.

Stephen burst out laughing when I said that, and I remembered then the pencil sketch I'd done from that photo in the *Gleaner*. It had never become the planned painting, but I still had it somewhere, probably in Veronica's scrapbook. Busta towering over Miss Princess on the dance floor, while Aunt Gladys looked on with a smile. She had nothing to worry about. A month later, she and Busta got married, and I was there, right there in the middle of the church. Ten years later, she came to my wedding too, when Connie and I got married up here in Kaya Bay. By then Busta was sick. He would have just another five years.

He died on Independence Day, I told Stephen. Almost like he planned it.

I asked Stephen if he wanted to see the scrapbook, but he said Chris had told him about it, so he felt he already knew the contents. He was much more interested in the art, and in the "historical work." That's what he called it. So I dug through to the back of the stack of canvases. I have so many. Maybe he's right, maybe I should sell some.

The last one I showed him is the biggest canvas in the studio. It's a life-sized portrait of Busta and Lady B., standing together, she in a patterned dress and he in a floral shirt. They both look happy in a quiet way, but also as if they're thinking about things, about the long way they've come. I'd taken my time with this one, painting each flower of the dress and the shirt. I finished it a month before she died but didn't get a chance to give it to her.

She was ninety-seven when she passed, I told Stephen.

I want to be your agent, Stephen said. Just think about it and let me know what you decide.

What did I have to lose? All right, I said. But some of these paintings aren't for sale.

CHAPTER TEN

Lists and Shirts

An ill-at-ease-looking young man sat in the kitchen with Aunt Della when Stephen returned from Kaya Bay. "This is Richie," Aunt Della said, as the boy sprang to his feet. He seemed about nineteen, lanky and awkward, with big eyes that stood out in his smooth face.

"Hi, Richie." Stephen shook his hand, wondering if he were the son of a neighbour, somebody he should recognize.

"Sorry bout yuh madda," the boy said.

Stephen stiffened. What did this boy know about him?

"Richie is the one who lick down Miss Pretty with his motorbike," Aunt Della said baldly. "He just bring us a whole heap of nice Julie mango."

Stephen exhaled. Oh, *that* mother. He could see the questions in Richie's eyes. Why had Stephen allowed his mother to roam the streets like a common madwoman? Stephen was on the point of saying, "She's not really my mother," but then thought it really was none of Richie's business. Besides, why had the boy been riding a motorcycle without insurance, not looking where he was going?

He asked this out loud, and Richie looked sheepish. "I get insurance now. I glad Miss Pretty don't press charges."

"Yes, you could've been in jail. What if she had died?" He was surprised at his own sternness, but there was just too much lawlessness and recklessness going on in the country. Uncle Alton's grief over his helper's death had affected him too.

"Luckily the fur coat kinda cushioned her," Richie said. "Is a good thing she was wearing it."

"Right," Stephen said in exasperation. He heard sounds coming from the staircase and rushed to help Miss Pretty descend, but Richie beat him to it, taking the steps two at a time to give the woman a hand.

"He came to visit her in the hospital too," Aunt Della said. "He's not a bad boy."

No, Stephen could see that. A phrase from long ago came into his head. It was Aunt Myriam at the children's home who'd said it: stupid people do more harm than wicked people. But Richie seemed to be neither, just young. Stephen wondered if he himself had ever looked so clueless.

Miss Pretty hobbled into the kitchen on her crutches and Richie helped her to sit down. "I bring you some mangoes, Auntie," he said.

Stephen rolled his eyes. He went over and squeezed

Miss Pretty's shoulder before moving her crutches to a corner of the kitchen, so no one would trip over then. That was one of the first things he had crossed off his list—crutches for Miss Pretty. But he still had a few other things to do before leaving.

Aunt Della washed and cut up three of the mangoes, and they sat round the kitchen table biting into the succulent flesh. Stephen knew he would eat more than he should and pay the price later with trips to the bathroom. But he couldn't help himself. What was it about mangoes? Sometimes in New York he bought boxes of them, more than he was able to consume, and then felt a feeling of betrayal when some rotted.

"Auntie, we need to do something about the roof," he said, when he'd had his fill and was washing his hands at the sink. "Before the rainy season comes again."

"What wrong with yuh roof?" Richie asked.

"It leaking," Aunt Della responded.

"All you need is some special tar," Richie said. "I can fix it for you."

Stephen stared at him. "What do you mean?"

"I know how to fix roof," Richie insisted. "That's what I do from time to time. But I looking for a real job. Things tough right now."

"What kind of job?"

"Maybe like in an electronics place. I can fix TV and all kinds of things."

Hmm-mmm, Stephen thought. *Jack-of-all-trades.* "You should specialise in one thing, and then do all the other things on the side," he muttered.

"Yes, I know," Richie said.

"That is good advice," Miss Pretty said in her succinct schoolteacher's voice, and they all looked at her. Every time she spoke, Stephen felt that frisson from her first comment to him all those years ago.

"Yes, but things not so easy."

"You have to find a way," Aunt Della said. "Maybe Stephen can help you."

There she goes again, Stephen thought, *putting me in the position of assistant-general.* "Well, you can start with the roof," he told Richie.

The next days were spent fixing up the house. Richie came with tubs of tar piled high on the back of his motorcycle in the morning, and Stephen helped him to climb onto the roof from the balcony, handing him up the containers. Aunt Della kept telling them to be careful as she and Miss Pretty watched them at work.

The sharp smell of the tar filled the air as the day warmed up, but Richie was done in a little over an hour. "That should keep the rainwater out fi now," he announced. He held onto the ledge that ran around the roof and let himself drop onto the balcony. He moved with such ease that Stephen wondered if burglary was one of his skills, but he pushed the idea out of his head. Féliciane always said part of his problem was that he didn't trust anyone, not even himself. But that wasn't true. He trusted Aunt Della.

"How long will it last?" he asked.

"Oh, it should be a'right." Richie was nonchalant. "I

goin give it a touch-up in a couple of months. If water come in before, Auntie can just call me."

"She has your number?"

"Yes, I put it in her cell for her."

Stephen nodded. He was pleased to see how Aunt Della had taken to the phone. He'd told her to go easy on the Internet, though, because the 4G could break the bank until he managed to get her a regular subscription. This, too, was on the list. But he could now tick "roof" off. Still to be done was the painting of the outside walls of the house, and Brandon had offered to help—for half what a professional painter would cost. Richie said he knew how to paint houses too, and Stephen was hardly surprised. Yes, jack-of-all-trades.

Later, as they sat in the kitchen, drinking the lemonade Aunt Della had prepared, Richie said, "I can ask you something, boss man?"

"All right. But the name is Stephen. I'm not your boss." He wondered what was coming—a request for cash, no doubt.

"No problem, boss. You know things tough down here, right? Job so hard fi come by, even when you willing fi work from morning till night. I been looking a long-long time."

"Yes, I know."

"So, what I want to ask you is—you think you can sponsor me fi go to America? I fraid of what might happen if I don't leave, all the shooting, all the gang ting."

"America? You serious? Sorry to disappoint you, man, but that is kind of beyond my powers." He hesitated, seeing the crestfallen look on Richie's face. "But, listen, what if I find a job for you here? You know my aunt need more help at the nursery and you could fix things up around the house from time to time. I can talk to other people, too, who want to come back to their house. What you think?"

"But who goin pay me?"

"We can sort something out. You just have to text me and tell me what you do each month, and we'll arrange things."

Richie nodded, looking doubtful, but happier than when he'd arrived. Afterwards, Stephen couldn't help wondering if Aunt Della had put the boy up to the whole thing; he dismissed the thought before it took hold.

The weekend before his departure, he, Brandon, and Richie worked for two days with rollers and brushes to give the house a new coat of off-white paint, while Aunt Della kept them refreshed with lemonade, coconut water, and patties she had made herself. Stephen's palms were sore at the end of it, but he was able to tick "paint house" off his list. Later he would take pictures for the website he planned to create, of Aunt Della's residence for artists. They still had to discuss the name. Jasmine would be the first "official" lodger.

As when he'd arrived, Stephen had to go round again to say goodbye to Miss Della's friends. He spent another half hour on Miss Vera's verandah, listening to her talk about Teena and her life as a teacher in Florida.

"I don't understand how pickney can behave like that at school," Miss Vera said. "Teena tell me bout how them facety, how she can hardly talk to them. I hope she find another job. Still, she getting paid more than if she had stayed down here."

Before he left, she told him she had something for him, and for Chris. She went into the house and brought out two short-sleeved shirts, one dark blue and one leaf green.

"The blue one is for you. Try it on and see if it fit," she instructed. He stood up on the verandah and put the shirt on over the tee-shirt he was wearing. The size was perfect.

Although he already knew the answer, he asked admiringly, "Did you make them, Miss Vera?"

"Yes," she said. "Of course."

When he took it off, she folded the shirt and put both garments in a paper bag that she handed to him. "Tell Chris thanks again for me."

Stephen didn't quite know for what, but he said he would. He then asked her a question that had been on his mind for years: "Miss Vera, do you know what happened to Miss Pretty's son?"

"Oh, the baby? She lose it after the car accident," Miss Vera replied. "Miscarriage. Just a month before he was to born."

"And the father?"

Miss Vera shrugged and raised her hands, palms upwards. "Who know? People say it was some white man. Water under the bridge. Miss Pretty have us now."

Stephen gave her a brief, awkward hug, and headed back up the hill for his last dinner with Aunt Della and Miss Pretty before he had to fly back to New York. He would come home more often, he thought.

part
three

CHAPTER ELEVEN

The Trees

I want to think it is over now, but I know the weather
just playing with we. The downpour start again before I can say "where mi umbrella," and the wind
making the trees bend left and right like a spite. I feel
sorry for them. Standing proud one minute, as if them
going be there forever, and the next swaying and shaking like them have no will at all.

Nothing to do but wait it out. Three days cooped
up in the house. The first day I sit at the machine and
work on the two dress that I making for Miss Della.
She need them for when she go travelling next month,
she say. First she going to New York to see Stephen and
then after that is big-big trip because Stephen taking
her to France. To Paris. What a excitement. She ask me
if I can take care of the house and all the dog-dem while
she gone, and I say of course, no problem.

Miss Della is the one who beg me to make the dress-
dem because although I sick of sewing, nobody can buy
in a store what I know how to make. It woulda cost

them nearly a whole month wages. When I finish with hemming the dress, I decide to do some housework, so I dust everything, even on top of the fridge. And I clean the stove and wipe all the grease from the wall tiles until them shining like new. Hard to believe how high grease can fly. I scour the bathroom sink after that and want to start on the tub, but I get too tired and mi shoulder start hurting like hell. Still, the house look damn good now, and I proud of meself because cleaning is another thing that I kinda let slip.

The second morning, I look outside and see the tree-dem pon the ground like dead body, and lawd-god-a-massy burst from mi mouth. I go out on the verandah and wave mi hand to Lorraine across the way, who also looking pon the destruction. After the landslide last year, is like bad luck just can't done. Lorraine raise up her arm-dem, like she asking: What to do? The rain still coming down, and Lorraine probably worried bout Miss Della nursery down the road. Every time flood and hurricane come, she have to start over with all the plant-dem. I sigh and go back inside. I spend the day folding up clothes in the chest of drawers, putting blouses together, sorting panties according to everyday wear and the one-dem for going out, folding up the cotton housedress Teena send me last month from America. I already tell her that I have enough, but every time she see one that she think I might like, she send it down with somebody coming to visit. So a stream of her friends always coming by, bringing me housedress from Sears or JCPenney. I know where they come from because of the tag. She take the price off but leave the tag on, maybe to show me that they brand new, she not sending me secondhand stuff. Not that I would ever think that. I wonder sometimes if she trying to tell me: Check out these dresses, Mommy, they nothing compared to what you can stitch up from scratch.

When I finish with the chest of drawers, I start on the closet, which is not in a bad condition since the things Albert did leave behind burn and gone already. Is a hell of a fire I light in the yard, even though the big-big flame-dem shooting up in the air didn't make me feel much better. Him clothes used to hang on one side and mine on the other side. Now some of Teena clothes, things I make for her, hang where him shirt and pants used to be. Teena like to keep a few clothes at the house so that when she come home on holiday she don't have to bring heavy suitcase. She moved to Florida only a few months after me and Albert separate, and when the divorce finalise, she ask me if I didn't want to come to America. But what I going to do there? I don't want to be a burden on her. And she say she don't want to come back right now because when she was here she was just boxing bread outta horse mouth, couldn't get paid right for all her hard work. Now she making decent money in one of dem-town near Miami, even if she have to get up at six and drive one hour to the school and one hour back. When we talk on the phone, she always telling me things bout her students, how nearly every day police come and have to cart off one of them in handcuff. I worry bout her, but when I look at her clothes-dem in the closet it make me feel like she not gone forever, that one day she going come home again and things will go back to normal. Sometimes I tell her that she should call Albert too, he still her father, but she say she don't feel like talking to him. Nothing I can do bout that.

The rain don't stop. On the third day I start looking through the bookcase, at all the book-dem that Teena used to use in high school. I take out *A Midsummer Night's Dream* and flick through it. I used to like reading long-long time ago, in elementary school. But when Teena little, is Albert who would read to her at night because I was too tired by then. Poem by Miss Lou. Things bout princess. I used to love hear him voice, that same voice that . . . but what the point of thinking bout that now. Albert always so sure him was the smarter one, but not too smart to stop him woman from calling me. Him used to joke that him have the brains and me have the looks. I didn't find the joke all that funny, but I way past all that now. I have mi own way of being smart. Not everything have to come from book.

I pull out a big green-cover one from the bookcase and open it in the middle. This one is old English. I did learn bout that in school. Is like yesterday and donkey years ago at the same time. *Paradise Lost.* I like the language, even if this kinda thing could give people headache. Anyway, enough with the book-dem. I decide instead to cook up a big batch of rice and peas, because who know when this damn rain going done.

But next day the sky clear and sun bright like nothing did happen. When I go outside on the verandah, I see him, the new man, another one of them artist people staying at Miss Della place. Last year she had a friend of Stephen staying with her for a long-long time, Chris him name was, painting flowers. Flowers every day and night until all her walls full of them. Everywhere she look is flowers. But they nice-nice. The first time I go up there to take a look, he give me one of the painting-dem as I leaving. See it right there on mi wall. But imagine, when Miss Della come down here to work at her nursery, she have to look pon even more flowers. I tell her that that woulda make me go nuts. But she just laugh. She love her plants to kingdom come, know how to make them grow and send out blossom like no tomorrow. When Albert go off, she bring me one plant that look all dry up like it soon going dead. Vera, she say, just keep watering it, take care of it for me. So I care for that plant like mi life depend on it, making sure it always have water, putting it in bigger pot, feeding it fertilizer. And look at it now, big-big croton on mi verandah, like mi best friend. Is yours, Miss Della say, when it come back to life.

This new man is from I don't know where, tall, bony, and kinda shy-looking, with a thin face and hair cut short. I think him maybe a little bit older than me. He walk round each tree lying there on the ground then bend down and run him right hand along the bark of one. Like him saying sorry or something. Him probably feel me watching him because him glance up at the verandah and him smile. I smile back. I would like to hang round and see what him plan to do with the tree but I have things to do. I have to go to the supermarket because the fridge look like I just buy it, brand new, not a thing inside. And I been longing for some fried sweet potato. Wish I had somebody to share it with, though, because one of the things that most make mi spirits drop these days is the eating by meself.

I take a quick bath and put on mi favourite olive-green skirt and blouse—another present from Teena—and I have to say I feel good that it still fit me nice. Mean that I don't put on too much weight, thank God for that. I been doing the exercise on the video-dem that Teena send down, and it look like they working. When I walk out the yard, I stop to look at what this carver-man doing, and even though he don't look up, I still say hello. Is like him hard of hearing, because is a full five second before him raise him head from scraping at the tree. Our eye-dem make four, and him look over the rest of me before coming back to mi face. But him not facety or anything.

Hello, Madame, him say, and I can hear right away that him don't really speak English, so maybe him language is Spanish or something. I smile and go bout mi business, wondering if him going to cut up the tree-dem and haul them way. I am sure them would lie there and rot before government send anybody to clear them up.

When I come back from the market, one of the tree-dem is a woman. It not quite finish, but I can make out the face and the bosom and the hips. She wearing some kind of wavy, meshy clothes. If I didn't know better, I would say she look like me. But I not going to fool meself. I look round for him, but him not there anymore. Probably too hot now for him to work in the sun. I walk along the tree, and can't help but laugh to meself. It must be nice to be able to do this kinda thing. Take tree and turn it into somebody.

I want to call to Lorraine to come out and look too, but I think she gone to help out Miss Della at the nursery already. She will see it when she come back to her yard.

The man turn up again the next day, and I watch him from inside mi living room. Him concentrate on the first tree, with knife and hammer and tool I don't know the name of. It burning me up to know what him doing, but I definitely not going to go out there while him still carving. Plus I have work to do. Besides finishing Miss Della dress-dem, I should start on the blouse that Lorraine been asking me to make for her. She give me the material long-long time now and while she not saying anything bout it, I know she kinda getting vex that nothing not coming. Everybody want me to sew, although I want to stop. I don't know where the love for it gone, but I find all sorta excuse not to sit at the machine nowadays. And is not only the knee pain, because that been around for a while and it never used to stop me. Today, though, watching that carver-man bending over the tree-dem, I feel like I should be making something too.

I cutting some silky material to make a waistband for Miss Della dress when I hear the gate creaking open, then somebody knocking on the living-room door. Of course, I always peep through the kitchen window before opening the door, because you never know, and is him I see standing there on the verandah.

Hello, I call out through the window.

Hello, Madame. Can I ask you for water?

All right, I tell him. Coming.

I open the door, and him hold back a little before coming into the living room. I tell him to sit on the high-back mahogany chair. I don't want him putting himself on mi beige sofa when him been working in the sun like that, with him shirt sticking to him body with sweat. And especially after all the cleaning up I been doing these last days. I go back through to the kitchen and take a bottle from the fridge and bring it and a glass to him.

You want some ice?

No, this is very good, Madame, thank you.

I like the way him talk, it sound so polite and educated. I can't remember anybody ever calling me *Madame* before.

I watch as him drink the water and notice the perspiration below him hairline and the grey in him hair. Looking at him up close like this, I think him must be bout the same age as me, or a little younger or older.

What you going do with the tree-dem when you finish? I ask him.

I don't know. I will probably leave them there. I might have to go home soon.

Oh. To which country?

Him tell me the name, and mi head full up with picture of river running bright-bright red with blood. That was the story in the *Gleaner* and on TV when them talk bout all the bad-bad things that happen in that country. I don't know what to say to him, but him smile at me and hand me back the glass.

Thank you so much, Madame.

Be careful, working in the sun like that, I tell him as him go through the door. And by the way, mi name is Vera.

Mine is Paul, Madame, Paul Mawenza. And him smile. And all of a sudden, is like somebody turn on light in him eye-dem.

I follow him on to the verandah and watch him for a couple minute as him start on the second tree. I wonder why him run him hand along the whole trunk before starting to cut.

I expect him to come again the next day and ask for water, but he stay outside working in the sun. So I carry the water over to him.

Him smile at me, looking grateful, and wipe him hand pon him pants before taking the glass. Him drink the water down in one go. I take back the glass then look good to see what him been up to.

This second tree now is a woman too, holding a little girl hand. The two of them have them hair in braids, ropy and long pon the wood. The woman have the same looks of the one on the first tree. I want to bend down to touch the wood, but I don't know if that would be right.

Nice, I say, before I leave him there in the sun and

go back to mi house. I think I going finish the first dress for Miss Della today.

People now coming down our street to look at the tree-dem and him working on the third one. Everybody have something funny to say. Because we live in a country where everybody is joker. But still you can hear that them admiring what him doing. Them just don't know how to say so. Is like when Albert left. I know people round here feel sorry for me, but nobody know what to say. If it was dead him dead, them would bring me food and sit with me pon the verandah, and hand me envelope with dollar bill to help take care of the funeral expense. But when man run off with other woman, what is there to say, really? Him gone to a better place? The angels taking care of him? Him in heaven now?

Still, when I put fire to all him clothes and things in the backyard, people come to look, like them doing now with the tree-dem. And is after that that Miss Della did bring me the dry-up plant. And she say to me, I always cutting off the bad parts of mi plants and burning them, and the next thing I know, the plant putting out new leaves and blossoms like nobody's business, and thriving. When she say that, I did just nod mi head.

I go out now and give everybody water to drink as them standing there in the sun, watching Mister Paul turn tree into whatever.

Heh-heh, the woman kinda look like you, Lorraine tell me. She standing behind her gate, taking in everything.

Me can't see the resemblance, I tell her. But if you say so.

I tell her that I going to start on her blouse soon, I just finishing up Miss Della clothes first, since she have to travel. And Lorraine say, Take your time, mi dear. But I know what that mean: You better hurry up before me get more vex.

When everybody gone, Paul come and knock on the door

You finish already? I ask him.

Yes, he say. Unless you have more trees, Madame?

Didn't I say mi name is Vera?

Oh, pardon me, he say, Madame Vera.

I can't help but laugh. Him have such a quietness bout him, and him eyes so kind and so—I don't know what—that I ask him if he want to have some of the rice and peas that I heating up.

With pleasure, he say.

So, we there eating, and I ask him bout the trees, especially the one with the lady and little girl. And he say it was him wife and daughter. And I don't want to push mi nose in him business, but still I ask what happen to them, although I already know in mi heart. And he tell me how a bunch of men chase them down. He don't go into any detail, but I can see what happen. I know what people can do with machete.

You remind me of her, him say, looking at me. Of my wife.

As we sit there, not eating anymore, him tell me that him have another daughter, a girl him adopt. She was a baby when him find her, lying on her own mother body. The people who kill her mother musta think she dead too. Or some little kindness musta got into them heart and make them leave her there. Him took her with him. Twenty-three years now since that day.

She will graduate from university next week, him say. So, I'm going back for that.

Oh. That is all I can say. Mi heart full and low at the same time.

But I would like to come back, him say, talking slow like him thinking bout things. I want to work on some more trees here. I think I will come back in July, if Madame Della has space.

I going to ask her, I tell him. I sure she will keep a room for you. And I going make sure storm knock down some more tree before you come.

Him laugh, and the sound full up the house, like fresh clean breeze after lightning and thunder.

CHAPTER TWELVE

Travelling Light

Christopher didn't know how the trip to France became a multinational family affair. He could feel people staring at them as they moved through JFK, with Miss Pretty in her fur coat at the height of summer. They were all there: his father, Stephen, Féliciane, Leroy, Miss Della, Uncle Alton, Jasmine—whom he was meeting for the first time, and whose brightly coloured hair attracted eyes like moths to fire—and Miss Pretty in fur with her walking stick.

The whole thing should teach him to keep his mouth shut in the future, Chris thought, because the madness had started with his opening up about his plans to go to Italy to visit Lidia's parents after they'd sent him an email asking him to come. They really longed to see him, they'd written, too much time had passed. And he should've kept the information to himself. But Féliciane had invited him over for dinner, and they were discussing the blockbuster Monet exhibition that had just opened at MOMA when he stupidly said, "I might stop over in France and visit the Monet museums before I go to Italy."

"What?" Leroy screeched. "You going to France? Féliciane, you hear that? If Chris going to France, I going with him. You can stay here if you want."

Chris had thought it was a joke, especially since it was the first time he had set eyes on Leroy. He liked the man, but he wasn't looking for a friggin' travelling companion.

"I need a visa?" Leroy asked. "You know, Fellie, if you decide to come, maybe we could get married there."

Chris had to laugh. "Whoa. Smooth, man. Nice way to propose."

Féliciane had stared at them both, looking as if somebody had sneaked up and vengefully stuck her with a pin. But once the curtains went up on his plans, there was no stopping the theatre piece. The next thing Chris knew, Stephen had got in on the action and arranged a group show in Paris, through contacts that Féliciane helped to provide. And the "group" meant not just him and Féliciane, but Uncle Alton and Jasmine as well. Later, Stephen claimed that it was Jasmine who called to ask why couldn't Aunt Della and Aunt Pretty come along as well, and she professed to be quite willing to take care of the paperwork on her end, apply for visas and the like. Of course, Stephen would have to get notarized documents that attested to the fact that both women were related to him, and that he had the means to be their sponsor in America. Stephen being Stephen would have said: No problem. You can always find a way.

Jasmine, meanwhile, would have to dress as a man when she passed through airports because her passport hadn't yet been changed. She told Stephen that her lawyer was working on it but that officials at the passport office seemed determined to block things at every stage.

Later, Chris's father joined the ensemble, saying he had always wanted to go to France and Italy and would love to see Lidia's folks. His father had started speaking more and seemed less forgetful since the operation. He now looked at Chris when he addressed him, which was a change from past years. During the time Chris had been taking care of him, they ate meals together, and went for short walks around the neighbourhood. One late afternoon, after they'd had coffee at the fancy new Filippo's on Second Street, his father drained his cup and said out of the blue, "I'm sorry, you know, Chris. I should have been more supportive of you, of your work. And after Lidia."

Chris was so moved by the apology that it took him several seconds to reply. "It's all right, Dad. I could've talked to you more about things."

When his father said he wanted to accompany him to Europe, Chris gave up on his plans to travel alone, and allowed himself to be carried along, with Stephen directing the show. He concentrated instead on finishing a series of dahlias that he wanted in the exhibition. He was proud of how good he'd got at this. If only Lidia and miss moon shine could see him now.

On the plane to Paris, they took up nearly a whole

row. Leroy had a window seat, with Féliciane sitting between him and Stephen. Across the aisle, Chris sat next to his father, while Aunt Della and Miss Pretty completed the four-seat section. In the next three seats, Uncle Alton was beside Jasmine and they seemed to be having a grand time, he laughing at her jokes and she tilting her head to listen to his stories. On Jasmine's right slept a man who'd donned his sleeping mask and leant his head back against his little pillow as soon as the plane took off. Stephen followed his example and inhaled deeply, trying to relax, but sleep came only intermittently. He kept hearing snatches of their conversation in his disturbed dreams. Stephen saying: I can share. We can work something out. Miss Pretty asking a flight attendant if she could walk up and down the aisle. The flight attendant saying yes, as long as the *Fasten Seat Belt* sign was off. His father informing Aunt Della that he would choose the fish and potatoes option and not the chicken and rice because he couldn't stand rice. Earlier, the flight attendants had distributed the menu, in English and French, and Chris had been surprised at how many of the French words he already recognized, from the lessons that Féliciane had given him. He knew it wouldn't be a language he would ever speak fluently, however, because the masculine and feminine thing drove him nuts. He told Féliciane he would just put "la" in front of every word, unless the word began with a vowel. "La" rolled off the tongue with ease, not "le." La pomme, la femme, la tête, la mère. He saved one "le" for "père," father, because Féliciane had insisted on that.

Chris felt lucky to have an aisle seat as he could stretch out his legs, but his father kept shifting, trying to find a comfortable position for his frame. He eventually changed seats with Miss Pretty, who then kept squeezing past Chris to walk in the aisle when there was no turbulence. By the time the plane landed at Charles de Gaulle Airport after seven hours, he wanted to strangle them all.

It was morning in Paris, but midnight body time and they all felt cranky and tired. Féliciane's dad met them at the airport, a slim man of medium height, with greying hair, dressed in a suit. He hugged his daughter and stroked her hair, then kissed the rest of them on each cheek, smack-smack eight times, with Chris and his father having to bend their heads for the salutation. He introduced himself as Jean-Marie.

"You 'ave all your things?" he asked. They checked their luggage, patted their pockets, and confirmed nothing was missing, and he ushered them to the taxi stand. Leroy, Féliciane, and Stephen would go in his car, and the others would take two cabs. He would meet them at the hotel, to drop Stephen off before taking his daughter and her partner home, where Maman was waiting. They got caught in traffic jams all along the highway, as the rush-hour frenzy clogged the way to the city. Chris fell asleep without trying and jerked awake only when the car came to a final stop, the driver getting out and slamming the door as he went round to the trunk to unload their luggage. He'd been surly and untalkative from the beginning, which had suited Chris fine.

Féliciane had found them rooms in a small hotel close to the Eiffel Tower and to the Seine. Might as well see the sights, she'd said. The place was a narrow, five-storey town house that looked as if it had recently been renovated, with varnished wood gleaming in the small reception area. They filled the tight space, standing with their suitcases, while Féliciane spoke in French to the solidly built man in white shirt, grey waistcoat, and black pants, who seemed to have permanently raised eyebrows. He switched to English and welcomed them with a joke, saying they had come at the right time for strikes, demonstrations, and other troubles, but that they shouldn't be afraid to explore the city. He showed them to the tiny lift, where there was room for only one person and one bag, and they creakily mounted to the rooms one at a time. The whole business seemed interminable to Chris. To keep costs down, they had opted to share two of the rooms—Chris with his father and Miss Pretty with Miss Della. The others had single rooms. Féliciane waited until they were all installed before heading off with Leroy and her Dad. She would come back to take them to lunch once they'd rested up.

From Chris's room, they could see the Eiffel Tower when they craned their heads from the window, and he smiled at his father's excitement.

"Can't wait to go up for the view," the older man said. But he was tired and stretched out on the bed after washing his face in the miniscule bathroom. Chris told him he planned to take a walk, and left him snoring in the room.

At the reception, he ran into Stephen, who had the same idea. They got maps from the raised-eyebrow man who said his name was Cléber, hence the name of the place—Le Relais Cléber. He was the owner and used to have a much bigger hotel. But he had to sell that one after his divorce, and downsize to this.

"Your room is okay? Everything's fine?" he inquired. They both nodded.

Cléber asked where they wanted to go, and reeled off recommendations of sights to see, telling them to be careful of pickpockets if they took the metro. Outside on the sidewalk, finally, Chris asked Stephen if he wanted to come along to the Musée de l'*Orangerie* where he was headed, but Stephen said he had things to do, gallery people to see, so they went in opposite directions, each relieved to be on his own. Chris followed Mr. Cléber's instructions and strode in the direction of the Eiffel Tower, through the dusty Champ de Mars park—a place for parades, concerts, and protests, Cléber had said. He'd warned Chris that things would be messy as the government was building a huge glass barrier around the tower to prevent terrorist attacks. You could no longer walk under the structure, as people had enjoyed doing for so long; you now had to go around, he'd said. Chris was surprised to see the throngs of tourists already out, a steady conga line of people heading in the same direction, their phones held aloft, snapping pictures of the tower. As he drew near to it, a group of about eight young men raced in his direction, shouting to one another. Chris pulled to one side, and they sprinted past, their eyes wide in fright, their voices hoarse. They were all dark-skinned, and the bags of trinkets they carried jingled as they ran, the scarves trailing behind them. Several tourists scrambled out of the way, as policemen on bicycles chased after the group.

Chris stared at the scene, overhearing a man say, "I don't see why they have to bother these guys. They're not harming anyone." And a woman, perhaps his partner, responded, "Yes, they're only selling souvenirs."

He turned to look at the speakers, and they gazed at him with friendly expressions, as if expecting him to join their conversation, to add his opinion. He nodded, kept his face blank, and walked on. He wondered how many times a day the chase played out, until it became just another weird game with the have-nots on the losing side. He felt empty, and not just because he hadn't eaten.

Skirting the Eiffel Tower to avoid the crowds, he crossed the Pont d'Iéna over the Seine and walked briskly along the Avenue de New York, passing the monument and the floral tributes to the princess who had died in a car crash in the tunnel beneath where he trod. He remembered how shocked his mother had been by the news—it seemed both long ago and still raw. "I can't believe it, I just can't believe it," she had said, shaking her head. "So young. And the poor boys." He couldn't avoid knowing that the second of the "poor boys" had got married not so long ago, since the ceremony had been beamed live around the world and had filled the newspapers from east to west.

He was perspiring by the time he got to the Place de la Concorde, where the expansive Jardin des Tuileries lay between the river and the gaudy Rue de Rivoli with its tourist traps. Cléber had told him to enter from the Seine side for the Musée de l'Orangerie, which housed some of Monet's famous water lily paintings. He mounted the steps to find that the museum was still closed and wouldn't open for another fifteen minutes. He stood indecisive for a few seconds, then walked around the gardens, looking out at the Luxor Obelisk and the fountain dominating the square and at the Eiffel Tower in the distance. He admired the shapes, composing a painting in his head that blended them into dark colours.

Strolling in the shade between the rows of trees, he passed people reading books on the benches, a family having a breakfast of baguette, croissants, and orange juice, a couple kissing as it were their last chance to do so—the woman sitting on the man's lap, facing him, her thighs around his hips, his hands on her waist—and girls taking photos of each other, with the river in the background. When he returned to the Orangerie, he was surprised at the long line and the security measures. It was almost like being at the airport again. But he'd read how things had changed after attacks in the city, that the authorities weren't taking any chances. As he stood in line to pass through the metal detector, he read the English version of the French sign above his head: *AT-*

TENTION! The big luggage, not entering the detector with X-ray, are not permitted in the museum, and cannot be left in the cloakroom. He was thankful he had no "big luggage," only his wallet and phone, which he had to put in the plastic container to be X-rayed. He walked through the metal detector, without any alarms going off.

The cashier handed him a brochure when he bought his ticket and he examined the plan of the museum. Downstairs was a collection with a double-barrelled title; it'd been generously donated by a woman who'd wanted the names of both her first and second husbands included for posterity, he read. The first husband, Paul Guillaume, had been the real connoisseur, "specialising in African arts, which, at that time, were a source of inspiration for avant-garde painters," said the brochure. Guillaume supported Picasso and acquired works by all the bold new artists of the 1920s. The second husband, Jean Walter, had been a rich architect and industrialist whose money boosted the expansion of the collection before his wife "ceded it to the State in 1959." Chris decided to see the collection first and put off seeing Monet's water lilies, the *Nymphéas*, for now.

At the bottom of the wide steps, he read more about the collection before going through to look at what the museum called "masterpieces in the history of art." To show the influence on the artists, the curators had arranged three African sculptures in glass cases—one from Ivory Coast and two from Gabon—and he stood gazing at these, with the Picassos in the background. Maybe everybody got something from somewhere else and there was nothing new under the sun, he thought. The brochure said that Guillaume and Picasso came together because of their "shared interest in primitive art and in particular 'negro' art," and Chris remembered Féliciane complaining that she didn't like going to museums because when she went as a child with her school, she didn't see herself in the exhibitions—no brown people, no women. As he stood in front of a painting of a young black man in a white shirt and black pants, playing a mandolin, he wondered if the curators were now making a special effort. He noted the title, *Le Noir à la mandoline*, by an artist he'd never heard of before, André Derain. He promised himself to find out more about him, and to ask Féliciane if she had seen these works. He could hear her voice in his head: Le Noir, La Noire. Black. Masculine and feminine. Colours. And people. He wondered how she might have felt as a French schoolgirl reading about "primitive" art.

Farther along the wall, he saw a portrait of the woman behind the collection—Madame Paul Guillaume, by Derain again. She wore a big yellow hat and an ivory dress that reflected the light. Chris stood back from the painting in appreciation and checked the brochure to see if Madame had her own first name. No, she was just referred to as "Wife." Later he would see on an explanatory panel that she was called Domenica, and for some reason the name stuck in his mind.

He strolled past the Modiglianis and stopped to examine Renoir's *Bouquet of Tulips*. Yes, he could do that now, paint flowers that looked like flowers, add the right amount of white to send the light streaming back at the viewer. Both Lidia and miss moon shine would probably agree. But he was still waiting for the light to stay with him, beyond the technique, even after all the canvases.

He spent nearly an hour taking in the collection, then bounded back up the stairs for the water lilies, first "presented to the public in 1927," when they attracted little attention, he read in the leaflet. As he stepped into the vast oval-shaped vestibule, he held his breath. Lidia had told him about these panels. She'd seen them in the months after 9/11, when she'd left New York and returned home to visit her parents. She'd spent weeks backpacking through different cities, trying to decide what she wanted to do after turning her back on finance. These huge paintings of lilies on the water—with their pastel mauves, blues, yellows, greens, and the reflections of the sky—had filled her with hope and lifted her depression, she'd told Christopher. They had spoken of coming back here together one day. He understood her awe now, despite the crowds. He stood back to take a picture, but people kept moving in front of him.

"It's difficult with so many visitors, isn't it?" The man who addressed him had red hair and wore a loose white shirt, black pants, and a patterned neck scarf. A badge hung from a ribbon round his neck.

"Do you work here?" Chris asked.

"Yes, I keep an eye on things."

"Are the paintings all real, or just copies?"

The man laughed. "When the paintings were brought here, they were glued to the wall. So they've never been moved. I've been working here twelve years now, and they've definitely been here the whole time."

Chris looked at the people milling around. Many were Asian women, dressed stylishly in frocks and hats as if they came from some of the portraits he'd seen downstairs. He visualised Lidia among them, in a patterned dress and the straw hat she used to wear in summer.

The man followed his gaze. "Monet adored the Japanese, and the Japanese adore him too. Lots of Chinese and Koreans are now coming as well."

They spoke for a while, and the man asked Chris where he was from. Chris told him and gave his name.

"My name is Shafai," the man said in turn, sticking out his hand.

"Cool name," Chris smiled, as they shook hands.

"It's Algerian. I came to France when I was very young, so I guess I'm neither French nor North African. I don't really know the Maghreb. I consider myself a terrien."

Chris wasn't sure what that meant, but he mentally translated it as "citizen of Earth." "Me too," he said. "But sometimes I feel like an extra-terrien."

Shafai laughed again. "You have to come back on a calmer day," he said. "Thursday and Friday are the best days. Forget the weekend."

Chris promised to return and shook Shafai's hand once more before leaving the atrium.

Outside the sun shone so bright it hurt his eyes, and the Seine acted like a mirror, reflecting the buildings along its banks. He saw that the cruise boats were already packed with tourists, and he could almost feel their exhilaration at being in the city, as a guide spoke through a loudspeaker, pointing out the sights in English and French. Chris descended the steps, crossed the Quai Aimé Césaire, and walked over the wood flooring of the pedestrian bridge—the word "pretty" popping into his mind. On the other side, he saw that the bridge was called the Passerelle Léopold-Sédar-Senghor, and the name rang a distant bell. Senghor, Senghor. Senegalese president? Yes, the sign said so. Président de la République du Sénégal. He'd ruled for twenty years. Chris readily acknowledged to himself that he wasn't one for history, yet this was another name he would look up.

His phone rang as he glanced left along the bank and saw a huge red sign with the letters *M O*. It was Féliciane calling.

"Hey," she said. "How's it going? I'll come get you guys in about an hour for lunch."

"I'm not at the hotel," he responded. "I'm out seeing your great museums." He told her where he was. "I guess M-O means Musée d'Orsay?"

"Yes. Lots of impressionism. Lots of light. Just your kind of thing."

He chuckled. "Can you give me an extra half hour? I'll meet you at the hotel."

"No problem," Féliciane said.

"By the way, everything okay?" He remembered how tense she'd been about the trip, about coming "home."

"Oui—oui. Everything's fine."

"And how's Leroy?" he ventured. He didn't want her to think he was poking his nose in her affairs.

"Oh, he's having fun. My mom loves him. He just fixed the kitchen tap which apparently has been dripping for a long time. My father isn't good at things like that . . . See you in a bit?"

"Yes. A très bientôt." He was proud of himself for remembering the phrase. Perhaps he should devote more time to learning the language when he got back to the States, he thought. Lidia had spoken it fluently, along with English, Persian, and Italian. You just have to set your mind to it, she'd said. Some words she never translated though. Firenze was always Firenze, never Florence. And he found he couldn't call the city by any other name, though he wondered what it would be in French. Perhaps the same as in English, but different pronunciation.

The queue to buy tickets was even longer at the Orsay, and he scrutinized the other people as he inched along. A tall blonde woman in a very short pink dress, with a tattoo of a strawberry on the back of her right leg. A balding man in flip-flops, his toes bony and twisted, the nails in need of a trim. Two thin Asian women with enormous white bags that screamed *CHANEL* in black letters. A lanky African American woman and her short white friend, giggling together, both seemingly delirious to be in the museum.

"Well, we're gonna do all the art," the first one said cheerily in her unmistakable Southern accent, which took Chris back for a moment to his Alabama childhood. He felt a surge of warmth that people travelled to see art, and he wondered what the woman would do if he went up and hugged her. She looked back, saw him watching her, and flashed him a smile. He winked clumsily, and she returned to her happy chatter with her friend. She probably thought there was something wrong with his eye.

Signs pointed to a restaurant on the top floor and he realised that he hadn't eaten in hours. He took the lift up and entered the Campana café with its huge golden chandeliers in the form of bells. A suited waiter came over, and he ordered a cappuccino and carrot cake. Inside the chandelier above his head, he noticed the pieces of metal, in different shapes, that had gone into the construction. Lidia joined him at the tiny square table, sitting on one of the blue-green chairs.

Look at that, she says, pointing to the huge round glass clock built into a wall of the café, letting in the light which frames her face and hair.

This used to be a railway station, back before the war, she tells him, and he smiles, impressed as always by her knowledge. He reaches across and takes her hand, as the waiter returns with a tray.

The carrot cake turns out to be inedible, dry and chewy as if it has been cut from a loaf that spent too much time in the freezer.

Never order carrot cake in France, Lidia laughs. You should've listened to me.

Words bubble up for a reply, but he swallows them. "Talking to yourself, Chris, is the first sign of madness,"

Lidia used to tease when she saw his lips moving as he painted.

After his snack, he stepped out onto the platform outside the café to admire the view, amidst the other tourists—of the river and the distant Sacré-Coeur Basilica, standing out like a monumental lighthouse. Picasso and all the others had spent time around the church, in the hills of Montmartre, loving its rough atmosphere. The area was on his list of places to visit before he and his father set out for Italy.

In the main Orsay gallery, he came face-to-face with two paintings that both Lidia and miss moon shine had worshipped, and he recalled the slides his teacher had shown in art class. They were opposite each other in the museum, Manet's *Le Déjeuner sur l'herbe*, with the nude woman picnicking with fully dressed men, and Monet's massive panels of the same name, depicting a glamourous group in a garden or park.

"That's how to know your Manet from your Monet," miss moon shine had informed her students. "Look out for the naked lady. And then the flowers, the water lilies."

But Manet must have liked flowers too. Chris took pictures of his *Pivoines*, wondering what the word was in English, and then of Monet's *Chrysanthèmes*. Looking at the paintings, he thought of Lidia's take on reincarnation: "I think that when you go, you know, Chris, the most you can ask for is to come back as a flower." And he'd always replied: "The end is the end. There's no coming back, Lid."

He rushed through the rest of the collection, conscious of the time and the agreement to meet Féliciane for lunch. He paused, though, before a portrait of a woman sitting in a garden, sewing, against a backdrop of scarlet blooms which he couldn't identify. Maybe tulips. She was wearing a white dress, naturally. The tag said: *Young Woman Sewing in a Garden*. It was by Mary Cassatt, the first woman artist he'd come across on this floor. Another one to mention to Féliciane.

Before he left the museum, he went back to look at the one painting he'd tried to avoid, the one he'd tried to walk past with his eyes averted: Monet's painting of his dead wife. *Camille sur son lit de mort*. Her blurred face was surrounded by streaks of light emanating from her shroud. The work caused Chris's stomach to cramp, and he rushed down the stairs, out into the fresh air and sunshine.

On the way back to the hotel, he took narrow, shaded streets and came onto a quiet garden-square dominated by an imposing neo-Gothic church, its twin towers stretching into the air. He sat on one of the benches in the garden for a short while, looking at the shapes of the church: the arches, the spires, the bas-relief figures on the façade. If Lidia had been there, they would've been holding hands, talking about the paintings they had just seen. He would tell her, laughing, that miss moon shine had once suggested that he might like to study architecture, and he had in fact taken a couple of elective classes, enough to enable him to recognize a building like this, built in the 1800s to resemble an earlier style.

He looked at his phone to see if he had enough time to go in and decided that he could take a quick visit. But first he logged into his email, searching for the last address he had for miss moon shine. *I've seen the Monets,* he typed. Before he got up to leave the garden, her answer came back, as if she'd been waiting to hear from him: *Good. Now you can forget his ass and do your thing.* She hadn't changed.

Inside the church, he was struck by the light coming through the stained-glass windows, casting psychedelic designs on the walls, splashes of blues, reds, pinks, greens. The church was empty, and he ambled down the aisles, examining the stations of the cross, the clothing and faces of the figures in realistic detail—folds in the robes, sculpted feet in sandals, even if one foot looked like it had six toes. Some of the wall paintings, by an artist named Lenepveu, had lost swathes of their story and were being restored, he read on a panel. He admired the *Conversion of St. Valerie and Her Mother Suzanne*, depicted in glowing detail. He'd never heard of either.

He sat on one of the low chairs in front of the altar, realising that he now had company. He heard the child before she appeared with her young mother, both speaking Spanish. The little girl seemed about five and gave off tangible energy in her pink dress as she looked excitedly around. Chris imagined that she saw the church, with its brightly coloured windows and pictures on the walls, as a kind of funhouse, and he observed that her mother was trying to hold her back from racing through the aisles. He smiled at them as they went past;

they both smiled back, the little girl looking at him in frank curiosity as if she wondered why he was alone. A few minutes later, a man who seemed to be in his late fifties trod up to the chairs, knelt, and briskly made the sign of the cross. He closed his eyes, and his lips moved in prayer. Chris looked away in embarrassment. Watching another person pray was like peeping at someone swimming in the nude or taking a piss against a tree. He got up and walked back down the aisle, trying to identify the characters in the stained-glass windows. He dropped some coins in a container and lit two candles, one for his mother and one for Lidia. Then he left the church.

He stood outside looking first at his phone, and afterwards at Cléber's map, to orient himself. He had only twenty minutes to make it back to the hotel. He heard the door creak open behind him, and the man who had been praying joined him on the steps, facing the garden-square. He lit a cigarette, and seeing Chris glancing at him, offered him one too. Chris shook his head no, muttering "merci."

"Vous venez souvent ici?" the man asked.

"Sorry, my French is not too good," Chris responded.

"I haven't seen you here before." The man's English was near perfect. "Are you a member of the church?"

"No, I'm just visiting."

"You're American?"

"Sort of. Citizen of Earth. Terrien."

"So, you're religious?"

"Not really," Chris said. What was his religion? Maybe art.

"Me neither," the man told him. "But it makes me feel better to come here. I pray to get rid of the hate."

His words surprised Chris.

"My son. He was gay. They beat him up in a bar, just for that. He died five months ago."

"I'm sorry," Chris said. Did he have the kind of face that people needed to tell him these things?

"So I pray for them. And for me and my wife. She's still very, very angry, and it's killing her."

"I hope they go to jail," Chris said.

"Yes. They will spend a long time in prison. But it won't bring my son back. And we have to go on. We have to try to understand why people do terrible things."

"Why the fuck should we try to understand?" The words erupted before Chris could stop them.

"Pardon?" The man looked shocked.

"I'm sorry. I was thinking of . . . something else. You're right, we have to try."

Chris didn't know what else to say, and the man changed the subject: "Enjoy Paris. It's a beautiful city." He dragged on his cigarette and blew the smoke out into the sunlight. Chris saw a bunch of roses in the puffs and closed his eyes briefly. He was tired. Tired of flowers, of seeing them everywhere.

The man trudged down the stairs, his back stiff, as if he were holding something tightly inside, and Chris followed slowly. He was going to be late meeting Féliciane and the others at the hotel.

CHAPTER THIRTEEN

Water Lilies

We all waiting in the tiny lobby of the Cléber hotel when Chris come back. Him look like him was rushing to get here on time, because him face full of perspiration. And him look sad too.

Sorry, everybody, him say. Then him turn to me specially, like I'm him mother. Sorry, Auntie D.

Is all right, darling, I tell him, so touched him calling me *Auntie* probably without even realising it. You here now.

When you reach a certain age, what is the point of rushing and getting worked up? Life too short and we all soon gone.

I tell him to take a few minutes to go up to the room and freshen up. When him come back down, we say to Mr. Cléber, See you later, and we set out, like a bunch of school-pickney going on outing. Nearly all of us hungry, and Jasmine saying that her stomach making noise like motorbike because she didn't have a crumb to eat since our flight.

Don't worry, Féliciane say. The restaurant is not far, and you'll love the food.

It look like Féliciane and Leroy have big breakfast, though, because Leroy going on about all the different kind of pastry him eat—éclair and brioche and whatnot. Him surprise that I know what him talking bout, but I did do a little French in school, long-long time ago. Never did know that I would make it to this country, though. But look pon me now, thanks to Stephen.

Leroy saying, That pain-au-chocolat thing—that's the name of it, right, Fellie? That is definitely mi new favourite food.

We laugh. Then Leroy ask Chris where he went in the morning.

So Chris start telling him bout all the museum-dem, while I listening with one ear. I glad to see Chris looking more relax. I worry bout him the same way I feel for Stephen. Like we is family. And I thinking: Look at me who never have nobody. And yet all of us is here like we on some big family reunion trip.

Is a short walk to the restaurant, and we pass building that look like them been here forever and then this big-big school for military people that stretch from one street all the way over to the next. Féliciane telling us bout everything we see, and I taking in all the information and using mi new phone to snap picture. I like this phone so much, and I so happy that Stephen get it for me.

While we walking, Féliciane keep bending down to pick up things from the sidewalk. A black hair band.

A gold button that musta left somebody with a spare buttonhole. A feather that is so bright-bright pink, I'm wondering what kinda bird it come from, or maybe it is from a toy. Féliciane drop all of them in her little cloth bag. Stephen already explain to me what kinda art she do, so I know this is for her work. But still, bending down and picking things up off the sidewalk like that don't seem right, and Leroy tell her so.

Mind the dogshit, you hear, Fellie? Leroy say. You could get some on your hand.

And Jasmine say, Bwoi, looks like this place have whole heap a dog, eh? People don't complain about the mess?

Too many other things to complain about, Féliciane tell her. Just walk like you come from here. Stare straight ahead and ignore whatever you step into.

Some people not staring straight ahead though. They looking at us, and especially at Miss Pretty and her fur coat. But Miss Pretty walking with her head up, holding on to Stephen arm, and Stephen doing like I tell him. Just act the son part. It not that hard, and it mean the world to her. I don't know if Miss Pretty really believing now that Stephen is her son, but it don't matter. Like I say, we not here for long and a little kindness don't hurt anybody.

We soon reach the restaurant. It on the ground floor of a building that is bout five stories high, and the front have design like somebody old country house, with door and window paint white. *Aux Créoles,* the sign say. Beside the door is a big wicker basket full of fruit. Nice ripe-looking mango, three banana, two orange, a sweet-sop, and one big fat pineapple that look like it just pick. I want to lift it up and smell it to see if it real, but I don't want to embarrass anybody.

As soon as we step in, this tall man with a big-big smile rush over and give Féliciane two loud kiss, smack-smack. She say something to him in French and him bust out laughing, then him turn and shake everybody hand.

Bienvenue. Welcome. I am Jacques, him say. Friends of Féliciane are friends of mine. Your table is ready and waiting for you.

I look around the place as Jacques lead we to a long rectangle table in the middle of the restaurant. The wall-dem full of painting, of flower and beach and such thing. Is like we at home. Chis looking at the painting too. They could be something he would do. But in the corner of each one is a curly *F*. And all of a sudden, the thing click: must be Féliciane do them. I see Chris when he reach out and give Féliciane a pinch on her arm. She look kinda surprise, and then she notice that Chris looking at the painting-dem. She smile, like she embarrass.

You? Chris say.

Yes, Féliciane tell him. Once upon a time. I do know how to paint.

Then Stephen jump in: What, these are yours?

Is Jacques who answer for her: Yes. She did them when I started the restaurant. She was a student then. I paid her with meals for weeks.

And I really think I got the better deal, Jacques, Féliciane say.

Lovely work, Jasmine say, like she bored. Then she
bust out, Lawd, I'm hungry.

Yes, all of we hungry.

Féliciane tell us that Jacques grow up in Martinique and
live all over the world after that because France own
country from South America to Pacific. Now Jacques
serving all kinda food from places him did pass through.
Red beans inna coconut milk. Fry plantain that taste
like them have sugar on them. Yellow rice. Salt fish frit-
ter. Curry lamb. And specially for Jasmine, a big-big
bowl of green beans, fry up with garlic. Chris and me
pass round the serving bowl-dem, and I have to smile
when I see how everybody dig in. Thank goodness that
Féliciane didn't take us to some fancy place where they
give you huge white plate with tiny-tiny piece of green
or yellow something.

The only one not eating fast is Miss Pretty. She sitting across from me, straight up like royalty, and moving
each forkful of food like she in slow-motion movie. The
dreadlocks hang round her face, and they hide what
happen all those years ago. Is funny, though, the longer
you know her, the less you see the marks.

So, how did you like the impressionists? Féliciane
asking Chris, while we all scraping our plates.

Loved them. And I was envious. Those guys could
paint flowers.

You're getting there, Féliciane tell him. Don't worry.

Sometimes the way she look at Chris, I wonder if she have feelings for him, just like the feelings I know Stephen have for her. He can't hide it. And Leroy also in the picture. Still, is not my business. Them going to have to work it out themself. I never believe in all this love stuff. I know people wonder bout me mi whole life, but I never been really attracted to man, or to woman for that matter. I did have one boyfriend when I was in mi twenties, and that cure me forever. I still get vex when I think bout that man and him bad ways—another story for another time.

By the way, Féliciane, Chris saying, do you know anything about this Madame Domenica Guillaume that I saw at the museum? She apparently bequeathed a lot of artwork to museums. Kinda inspiring, right?

Oh, her! You know, she was suspected of killing both husbands and attempting to murder the second husband's son, so she had to give all the precious artwork to the state to avoid prison. Féliciane laughing as she say this.

Really? Chris say. Wow.

I don't know who they talking bout, but I find it funny that you can give government artwork and escape going to prison. Wouldn't work at home. Better try whole heapa cash.

All of we love the dessert Jacques serve. Is a spongy cake soaked in brown rum, and I swear that I going try this when we get back, even if baking not really my thing. As soon as we polish it off, Jacques come back to announce that we can have any cocktail we like, on the house. Féliciane tell me I might like the coconut punch, and I decide to have that. It nice so till. While I sipping, Féliciane tell us bout the plans for the next day. She going to collect us early at the hotel with a minivan, and we going to Giverny. This is where the artist Monet used to live, and it full of the water lily that inspire him painting. I don't really care so much bout the painting-dem because mi house still full of the artwork Chris leave, but I want to see the water lily and all the other plant and flowers.

I ask Féliciane what exactly growing in the place, but she say is a surprise for tomorrow.

Now I'm imagining all kinda big-big pond with water lily. The first time I see this sorta plant was at Hope Gardens, long-long time ago, when I was on a school outing. Thirteen or fourteen years old, and I didn't know one thing bout plant even though I grow up round them. But this lady at Hope Gardens take us round, telling us the name of everything, what kinda care they need, and where they come from. I still remember her name. Miss Fletcher. And then she bring us to the pond, with these plants just so nice and peaceful, lying there on the water, and you could see the sky, and the cloud-dem, as if the water was mirror. And is like something touch me. I couldn't tell you what though.

Is after four p.m. by the time we finish lunch, and we the only one left in the restaurant. As we go out, Jacques kiss all of us, even the man-dem, and I can see some people uncomfortable.

Me no like man kissing me, you know, Leroy say when we walking down the street.

Lawd, just be quiet, Jasmine tell him. Féliciane raise her eyebrow, but she don't say anything. For the next hour, she take us on a tour round the neighbourhood, showing us a whole bunch of café and church where famous writer and artist used to hang out. I know some of the name-dem. And for the other ones, is the first time I hearing bout them.

Next morning, we drag ourself out of the bed and go downstairs for breakfast. Well, if you can call what Mr. Cléber serve breakfast. Piece of bread with too much butter and jam, and coffee or tea. I go for the mint tea because this kinda breakfast will give you gas, and is only mint or ginger that can prevent this.

Give me boil-banana and mackerel any time over this, right, Chris? I say, and he laugh.

Miss Sheila used to make such a wonderful breakfast, Uncle Alton say. Then him face get cloudy and him stop drinking and put him coffee cup down. I know that him still miss him helper, and I feel for him. It was a terrible way to go. I hope none of us have a departure like that.

We'll buy you some mackerel over at Monet's house, Chris say, and Uncle Alton manage a little laugh.

Féliciane and Leroy turn up right at eight thirty, and all of us get into the minivan, full up of excitement. Féliciane look like a good driver, the way she manoeuvre the van down the narrow street-dem and out of our

Cléber tourist neighbourhood. She concentrating on her driving while Leroy talking up a storm, telling us bout all the nice things he had for breakfast at Féliciane mother and father house.

That croissant with almonds. You shoulda taste it. And the éclair. Bwoi, it nice. I think I want to stay in this country.

I catch Leroy looking at Stephen, but Stephen staring out the window, ignoring him.

Is a surprise to see how quick we out of the city and in what look like country. As soon as we cross a third bridge over the river, we start seeing field and what must be hay, wound up neat like giant roll of toilet paper. Then high wheat stalk. And whole heapa cow, grazing on grass, and looking twice the size them should be.

Those are some impressive cows, eh? Chris father say. What kind of food are they eating?

Must be hormones, Jasmine laugh.

Look like they chewing some grass too, though, Leroy say. When I was a little bwoi, I used to love watching cows chewing them cud.

You come from country? Jasmine ask him.

No, I grow up downtown. But at a certain time, a few cow and goat used to wander round. I wonder what happen to them? People probably butcher them for the meat. Or they got shot.

The visitor carpark is almost full when we drive into the Giverny place, and Féliciane have to circle round, looking for a spot big enough for the minivan. After she park, all of we get out and stretch, feeling the jet lag. Then we join up with a whole bunch of people heading down this narrow road. Everybody following signs for the entrance to the garden. We pass little shops that selling painting and souvenir, and Jasmine want to take a look, but Féliciane say we can do all of that later. The queue already have bout forty people when we reach near, and everybody talking some different kinda language. We line up too. Meanwhile, Féliciane is digging round in her knapsack for the ticket-dem. She tell us that she order them online and print them out.

Okaaay, she say, like she just win a prize. Here they are. I was getting worried. Maybe we can go right up to the front as I think these people are waiting to buy their tickets.

So we move to the head of the queue and stand waiting for Féliciane to ask one of the attendant-dem bout what to do next. Before she can say anything, though, trouble start. This big red-face man in the line is looking Féliciane up and down in a real facety way.

Hey, where are you from? he ask her.

Féliciane stare pon him, face cold. France, she say. The way she answer would give anybody the hint not to ask her anything else, but the man determined not to get the message.

And where is your boyfriend from? him ask. Him flash a look at Leroy, standing there close to Féliciane.

La Jamaïque.

Oh my God, say the the man, as loud as him can.

That's too bad. I feel sorry for you. You know, those Jamaican guys like to fuck around. And they always want to jump the queue.

All of us staring at him in shock now, trying to think of something to say. But before Féliciane or Leroy can react, Stephen jump forward and grab the man by the front of him shirt. Then him draw back him right hand and crash him fist gainst the man jaw. And is like I rooted to the spot as I watch him push the man so hard that the fellow land on him backside in the dirt. Meanwhile, people shouting and scattering. And Stephen getting ready to do more, but Chris and Leroy holding him back.

I hear mi voice saying, Lord have mercy, Stephen. What get into you?

By this time, two guard-dem in black pants and shirt come out from inside and start shouting at the top of them voice.

Ça suffit! Enough now.

Féliciane trying to tell them something while they helping up the fellow Stephen hit, but they not listening. And it look like the fool-fool man want to continue the fight, but with all of we standing round Stephen, and Miss Pretty lifting up her walking stick, him back way, cussing.

Idiot, Féliciane call out after him.

Now a woman with bright orange hair is talking to the guards. That man started it, she saying. He was being offensive. It's not their fault.

Other people join in too, calling the man stupid and bigot and crazy and all kinda word.

So, the guard-dem let us go in. And we spend a good hour inside the place, looking at all the plant-dem, dahlia and rose and iris and more. And I see the water lily, all the different colour, with the reflection of the cloud and sky in the pond-dem, just like postcard. But still we not talking much, and everyone is kinda down, with Chris especially holding him face tight-tight. And I'm thinking that garden and flower not supposed to have this kinda effect. We silent even when we back in the minivan, until Jasmine all of a sudden start laughing.

Mister Ali, she calling Stephen. Float like a butterfly. Sting like a bee.

So then we all start laughing, except for Stephen. He barely smiling and I feel that maybe him hand hurting him. You can't crack a blow like that without feeling pain yourself.

You cool, man? Chris ask him, and Stephen nod, still embarrass.

He avoiding looking at me because he know that is not how I raise him. And though I was laughing a little while ago, I sad to realise that the dark space in him that I think was gone is still there. But maybe I have one too, if I look deep enough.

What disgusting words from that awful man, Miss Pretty saying now. Utterly disgusting. You did the right thing, son.

Is the first time she speaking since we leave the ho-tel this morning. And I don't want to disagree with her, but Stephen need to know.

No, he didn't do the right thing, I say. Next time

we just turn our back on fool-fool people like that.

Miss Pretty go silent again, and she draw her coat round her.

Then Féliciane say, Thank you, though, Stephen. I definitely couldn't have handled it myself.

And Stephen look even more depress.

The day not finish with we yet, though. We run into big-big police barricade on the way back to the hotel, all the officer-dem bulk up in riot gear. Féliciane lean out the window to ask them what going on, and then she say "merde" in a loud voice when them inform her.

Sorry. The chemises blanches, she tell us. I completely forgot.

Then she explain bout all the demonstrator-dem that been taking to the street for weeks, all wearing white shirt and demanding that government reform things and stop raising prices because some people so bad off. She say the whole thing start with fuel increase, and this remind me of all the riot-dem and roadblock we used to have every time gas price go up.

My dad told me to watch out, Féliciane say. But I completely forgot.

What's with the white shirts though? Jasmine asking.

Well, the demonstrators wanted loads of people to come out and they figured that everyone owns a white shirt or blouse. That way they stand out as a movement.

Hmm, I don't think I own even one piece of white clothing, Jasmine say. Not my colour at all.

My mom and dad joined them the first few weekends because, really, some things need to change. But they didn't like the violence, so they haven't been back, Féliciane saying.

It take her more than one hour to find a clear route to the hotel, and all this time we can hear sirens screaming everywhere.

When we walk into the lobby, Mr. Cléber say, Well, looks like you chose a rather bad time for your trip. If you want to go out for lunch, I would stay around here.

Later on television, we see the report-dem of smash-up shop window, car set on fire, water cannon, and tear gas. I go to bed full of worry, expecting not to get any sleep. But I'm gone almost as soon as mi head touch the pillow. And in mi dream, I'm a young woman, walking on water, jumping from lily pad to lily pad.

I wake up in the middle of the night, remembering that second time I go to Hope Gardens and see the water lily–dem. It was the time when I was living with that man, the one and only boyfriend. Even now it hard for me to believe I stay with him for so long. The man used to act like I belong to him, like if I want to talk, I have to ask him permission, like if I put on certain clothes, he have the God-given right to tell me whether them suit me or not. When the two of us was in the little apartment, it always feel like him was a vacuum cleaner, sucking up all the air and leaving none for me to breathe.

I meet him on mi first job, after I move to town. Those days I was tired of being in country, especially after Granny pass away and leave me alone in the house.

Maybe I was looking for somebody to lean on, and Derek musta fit the bill. Him was a big man, bout six foot, just a little taller than me. And him did look good and know it too. The supervisor assign him to train me when I start at the accounting office, filing things. At first, him seem so nice and gentlemanly. Is only later that I realise bout the nasty temper.

After a month, him ask me to go to see a show with him, and from then we was going out every weekend, to beach and thing. We go out for months before we start live together, planning to get married. And I leave the job because him say it was better that the two of us not working at the same place. It didn't take too long for the constant quarrelling to start, though, even if me is not somebody who like to fuss and fight. But every little thing set the man off.

One evening, we have a big argument because him say mi cooking don't taste good, when that is one thing I learn to do from when I little. Granny teach me everything bout food because is she raise me after mi mother go England. So I cooking like from the time I can walk. But that is the thing the man use for insult. When I tell him to start cooking for himself, him get up from the table and, bam, punch me in mi mouth. And the shock cause me to wail out more than even the pain, while him rubbing him hand like is him get hurt. I rush to the bathroom and see mi bottom lip split wide open and blood running down. I never so vex in all mi life. When I go back outside, him standing there, not even looking sorry.

That is what happen when you talk to me like that, him say.

I don't answer. I just get ice from the fridge and wrap it in a towel and put it on mi mouth. And when him go to bed, I stay out on the couch, thinking that maybe I should take a knife to him in him sleep. But I banish way the bad thought-dem. And next day when him go to work, I leave the house, not knowing where I going, mi face still swell up but not so bad. Ice is everything.

Somehow or other, I end up at Hope Gardens, so quiet that time of day. I walk round, past all the tree. I take mi time, looking at the yellow blossom-dem from the frangipani, the bright orange queen flower, the bull thatch palm. I remember all the name-dem from Miss Fletcher, even the Latin one-dem that she did tell us. Plumeria. Lagerstroemia speciosa. Sabal jamaicensis. That palm was one of the few that originate on the island, she did say. I look at it, how it standing apart and sturdy like anything. I walk some more, past bougainvillea and nutmeg tree, until I get to the water lily pond. And I sit down by the side, not caring if mi clothes getting dirty, looking into the water, feeling the funny feeling like the first time. And clear through the quietness, I hear Granny talking to me: I didn't raise you for man to come punch you. Take your backside out of there.

I go back to the apartment and pack up mi clothes. Then I throw a vase into the TV screen and fling all the glass and plate-dem onto the kitchen floor. The sound give me so much pleasure. After that, I take a bus to Parade and from there, another one to country, to the house and land Granny left me. The plant-dem provide nearly all I need. And after Stephen come into mi life, I never try to find anybody else.

Is a long time before I fall back asleep, just lying there listening to Miss Pretty snoring in the other bed. The jet lag must be catching up with me. I reach up and touch mi left breast. The lump not getting any smaller. I don't tell Stephen anything bout it yet. No point in worrying anybody.

Next day at breakfast in the Cléber, Stephen break the news—the art exhibition off. The gallery destroy and burn up in the riot. Stephen tell us the owner call him first thing this morning, and although she sound vex, clearly she one of these people who know that life must go on.

These things happen, Stephen say, imitating her. Nothing to be done.

He ask her what happen to the painting-dem and all she say was, Gone up in smoke. So very sorry.

Except she didn't sound that sorry, Stephen say. In fact, before she hang up, she make the comment that a little excitement could sometimes be good for every-one, and for art. At least that is what Stephen say he understand. A demonstration here, a riot there—life go on, and we have to go with the flow.

She must have a really good insurance policy, Ste-phen say.

And will we get reimbursed for our work? Jasmine ask him.

That might take a while, Stephen tell her.

Don't worry, Uncle Alton say. We didn't paint any-thing that we can't paint again.

Yes, right, Jasmine saying under her breath. Then she announce, I'm going out for a walk. Anyone want to come?

Uncle Alton get up first, and him and Miss Pretty trail after Jasmine, like chicken following them mother out the coop.

I'm going back upstairs to take a nap, Chris's father say. And him head for the tiny elevator.

So is just me and Stephen and Chris there now.

What is our plan B? Chris ask.

Look, man, Stephen tell him, I'll take care of things here. You go to Italy a bit earlier with your dad and see Lidia's parents. We'll meet back here for the flight home.

Chris look at him like he really not certain bout any of this.

Don't worry, Stephen say. I'll make sure everyone has a good time. That was part of the purpose for bring-ing Auntie Della and Miss Pretty here, and they're going to have the time of their lives. They deserve it. And this should've been just a vacation anyway. I work too much. I think I might even do a little sketching.

Cool, Chris say. You know, I've never seen any of your work.

He can draw good-good, I say.

Stephen reach over and hold mi hand and I squeeze his before he let go.

Auntie Della think I'm perfect at everything, he say.

Not everything, I correct him. And him and Chris bust out a laugh.

Okay. If you're sure you can manage, Chris say.

You talking to Mister Fix-It, I tell Chris. Don't forget.

As we go out the breakfast room, Chris is telling Stephen, with him voice low as if him think I'm hard of hearing or something, I hope it all works out with Féliciane.

And Stephen say, with false bravery: I can hear it. Oh, it will. She'll stay with Leroy. He knows how to fix taps. And I scare her too much.

You scare everybody, Chris say, laughing.

No, not Jasmine, and not Auntie Della, Stephen answer him. So, what do you want to do today, Auntie?

I think I want to go back and see the water lily–dem, I tell him. Maybe just you, me, and Chris this time.

—The End—

Acknowledgments

Heartfelt thanks to Superwoman Tanya Batson-Savage, a wonderful editor and publisher, among her many roles; to the great Kwame Dawes for all he does, and for asking: "Do you have a novella?"—which turned into a novel; to Johnny Temple and the Akashic team; to G, Djav, and Jade for their love, support, and untiring encouragement; to sculptor Alexander P. for his art; to gardeners and painters of flowers everywhere; to my family and friends.